HIGH-WIRED

The Fine Line – Volume One

Andrea Frazer

Published by Accent Press Ltd 2015

ISBN 9781783757701

Copyright © **Andrea Frazer** 2015

PROLOGUE

It had started with curses and insults, spitting and pushing; it had escalated into punching and then, when he'd finally collapsed to the ground, it had continued with kicking. The young man was finally reduced to the only defence left to him, curling into a foetal position on the floor.

Then all was quiet for a while, but when he uncurled his head and lifted his face to see what was happening, he got a fierce kick from a metal-capped boot that knocked out two of his front teeth. Spitting blood, he turned his head into his body again, only to hear a voice saying, 'No, not that.'

Risking a very quick peek out of his hedgehog curl, he was horrified to see one of the figures holding a blow torch. Holy God, surely they weren't thinking of using that on him? He had felt a rib or several cracking when the kicking had been at its height, and he was pretty sure his eye-socket had suffered damage from one of the early swings of an anonymous boot, for he had no idea who these men were. All of them wore ski-masks and none of them was careless enough to use names.

'Not his eyes, smackhead. We want him to see death coming for him: see its approach and smell its stench. Have you got the cross and the wire? Oh, you dirty bastard,' said the small one at the sight of their victim spitting blood again and, aiming another kick, he caught the young man on the head, making him drift into a semi-comatose state.

As he swam in and out of consciousness he was aware

1

of his arms being stretched out as two of them stamped on his hands with their heavy boots, and he heard, in his head, the sound of shattering bones. The blessing of darkness overcame him for a while.

Before he completely blacked out, he was aware that he had evacuated his bowels in his terror, and the draughts blowing through the derelict warehouse also declared that he had wet himself, as it made the dampness at his front noticeable.

When he next became fully conscious of his surroundings, he realised that he could not move his arms, and that they were restrained all along their length by something thin and sharp, cutting through the material of his woefully inadequate light jacket.

Someone grabbed one of his legs, and he tried to kick out with the other one, but that, too, was grabbed in a crushing grasp, the two limbs were forced together, and the binding of his legs began, from the bottom up, some of the others holding him down so that he couldn't hinder their progress.

'Has the hole been dug?'

'About midnight.'

'Let's get our little muppet into the ground then. As ye sow, so shall ye reap. I wonder who'll harvest this little triffid?'

As they lifted him, he was aware that he was tied – it felt like with wire – to a stout, cross-shaped object, that had the texture of wood, and they were carrying him horizontally towards a large van that was parked over by the big double doors.

Why had he obeyed this summons to come here? As far as he knew he had done nothing wrong. Well, nothing much that he thought would have been noticed. Just the odd skim here and there, and a few free samples – for personal use only. He had almost always obeyed the rules; there had been no grave transgression on his part of which he was aware, but he had not been given the opportunity to state his innocence.

He remembered how the figure had appeared out of nowhere, and his present nightmare had immediately started. At first he thought they were just going to rough him up a bit, but as it got more serious, he began to fear for his life. By this stage, as he was manhandled into the rear of the nondescript van, he was practically devoid of hope.

When the vehicle stopped, his incapacitated body was manhandled back out of the van and through a gate into a field, with a brief stop just after they had entered when he heard a couple of snips, and an evil chuckle of laughter from his prospective executioners.

His bound body was roughly dropped on the ground, and in the light of the moon, for it was a clear, cold night, he saw one of them approaching him with something round and spiky in his hands. Whatever it was, it was suddenly jammed over his head so that it rested on his forehead, impaling him with small spikes and leaving little trickles of blood, and he realised that it was a circlet made of barbed wire.

'A crown of thorns for our little martyr, eh, lads?' asked an evil voice with the ghost of schadenfreude *in it, and he was aware of being raised upright. For a millisecond it crossed his mind that they were going to let him go; that all this had just been a sadistic and cruel lesson from which he might learn not to try to do anything dodgy again.*

There was an agonising jolt that made the thrumming pain throughout his body positively sing, and he saw them all move away from him, blowing kisses and laughing, as at a hearty joke. Only this was no joke. Left completely on his own in what looked like the middle of a field, tears of frustration, pain, and fear trickled down his cheeks, and he wept for the life he had expected to live, and for what might have been: the injustice of it all, that he didn't even know why this had happened to him.

Surely he had been careful enough to keep his little bit of skimming and free samples hidden. Surely it couldn't just be because he wanted to leave? After all, he'd had enough, he'd even provided his own replacement, and they wouldn't be any the worse off for his 'resignation', if you could call it that? His senses were suddenly distracted at a puff of breeze, but all he could smell was blood, urine, and excrement. Surely this wasn't it? Was he really going to die here, in this lonely field?

CHAPTER ONE

'I've just had another dressing-down by that sod Devenish,' barked DI Olivia Hardy at her sergeant, Lauren Groves. Superintendent Martin Devenish, their superior, was based at their station, meaning it was hard to avoid one of his frequent outbursts of displeasure. 'And how come you always look so perfect, in your suits and matching shoes and handbags?' she asked, apropos of nothing, but curious as to why their appearance was always so at odds.

'I suppose it's just the way Nanny taught me to present myself,' replied DS Lauren Groves with a sympathetic smile.

'Nanny?' responded DI Hardy.

'Ooh, get 'er! Lady Muck personified,' jeered DC Colin Redwood, a young man who could be very irritating if he chose. And frequently did.

'Leave me alone,' said DS Groves.

'Yeah, get off her back,' Hardy joined in. She'd had enough of Redwood and his smart-alec attitude over the last couple of weeks. 'Anyway, we're celebrating winding up our first case together with a decent cup of coffee from that café next door.' Her demeanour improved as she re-focused on her successful case. 'And who rattled your cage anyway?'

As Redwood subsided, the phone on Hardy's desk trilled. She lifted the receiver and listened, still wearing her smug expression. She had wound up a very messy case of tit-for-tat gang crime and she felt good. Her good humour soon changed, though, to one of resignation and dismay.

With an abrupt movement of her head, she indicated to DS Groves that she should accompany her, explaining as she grabbed her coat and car keys that there had been a head-on collision on the ring road, and that it was going to be a messy one. 'You'll be good at breaking the bad news to the families – must be something to do with your posh upbringing, but it always seems to come better from you than me.'

'Thanks, ma'am,' replied the younger officer, easing any creases in the back of her skirt that she might have acquired sitting at her desk. 'I'll just get my handbag. But why have we been called out? Shouldn't Traffic be dealing with it?'

'In normal circumstances, but they think the guy who was alone in one of the cars is as high as a kite, and that there may be drugs in the car.'

'So what about the Drugs Squad?'

'Too far stretched, it would seem, so, for now, this is our baby. Don't whinge, it could be worse. It could be a punch-up in a pub at closing time with broken glasses and knives. Give me a nice, clean accident any day of the week – less chance of getting injured, or even murdered.'

'Can I come too, guv, please?' pleaded Redwood, but his ambitions were immediately quashed.

'You stay here and mind the phones like a good little doggy. You've got about as much tact as a breeze block, and you always look too self-satisfied to be comforting the relatives of the dead.'

As the two women left the office, Redwood offered an upraised middle finger to them and muttered, 'Sour old bitches.'

From the corridor came Hardy's voice. 'I heard that, and I don't approve of that sign. I'll speak to you about respect for senior officers when I come back, Detective *Constable*.'

Redwood slumped back into his chair and played with the pens on his desk. The DI never let him do anything interesting, and he was getting bloody fed up with it. For a few minutes he toyed with leaving the force and joining the army, but the thought of actually going off to war soon made him rule this idea out. He decided he'd be better off staying where he was – and anyway, his present position gave him some inside opportunities. Also, he had some other irons in the fire which could make him a lot of money with his nose for profitable sidelines ... 'How did you know what he was doing?' asked Groves.

'He always flips me the bird and mutters some insult when I tick him off, so I thought I'd employ that famous attribute that all mothers have – eyes in my arse – and bring him up short.'

'What do we know so far?' asked Groves, returning to the scene of the accident towards which they were heading, as the two detectives made their way out to the car park.

'Uniform and the ambulances are already there; three dead, one not far off, and one other with multiple injuries who'll have to be cut out of the car. Fire Service's on its way.'

'Oh, damn!'

'So, apart from not liking the sight of mangled bodies, how are you getting on in our happy little station?' Hardy asked, a slight hint of sarcasm in her voice.

'It's all right,' was Groves's short reply, but after a few seconds of silence, she continued, 'Is that Colin Redwood always so bloody rude? Excuse my language, but he really gets on my nerves.' She didn't really approve of swearing – and Nanny definitely would not have approved.

'Join the club, Sergeant. He gets up everybody's nose. Just ignore him and hope he'll put in for a transfer soon. What about the rest of them?'

'Well, I don't really know them very well, but they

seem a friendly enough bunch. The superintendent's a bit scary though, isn't he?'

'Only if you actually listen to him, and you take what he says seriously.'

They took a pool car, as DI Hardy wasn't willing to put any more miles on her own car's clock than necessary, nor did she want its immaculate bodywork put in any peril. Leaving the car park, she headed north to the ring road round Littleton-on-Sea to see what awaited them in the mangled-limb department.

'God, it stinks in here. Someone's had one or two sneaky fags when they've taken this out last. I'm definitely going to make a complaint this time. I don't care if it's pouring down with rain, they'll just have to find somewhere else to indulge in their filthy habit.

'I only gave up six months ago, and smelling their stale smoke is sheer torture. I don't know how I haven't cracked, in this job.'

Olivia Hardy was on the short side, and somewhat tubby. Her hair was cut short for convenience's sake, and she wore only mascara and lipstick as her warpaint to work. Her rotundity had increased since she had quit smoking, of which she was well aware, and she was always intending to do something about it 'next week', whenever that would be. Maybe. Her everyday attire was casual – *very* casual since her size had increased.

'My suit's going to reek when I get home,' replied Groves, not really listening. 'I'll have to drop it into the dry cleaner's tomorrow.'

Lauren Groves was always finicky about her appearance. She was a complete physical contrast to Hardy. Very tall – nearly six feet – naturally slim, and brought up never to be sloppily dressed, even in her own home. It really was just the way she'd been brought up, with a nanny first, then life at boarding school.

The police station they had just left was situated about

half a mile from the promenade, in the medium-sized coastal town of Littleton-on-Sea. The station had been built in the 1970s to serve an ever-growing population, and had been constantly added to in an ad hoc manner by the use of Portakabins and other 'temporary' structures.

At first glance the town itself gave a good impression, the road opposite the neat green by the sea lined with Georgian houses, once grand residences for the new middle classes and their live-in staff. Now, though, most were divided up into minuscule flats and bedsits, the facades faded and peeling.

At night, however, the dark underbelly of the place began to show. Situated on the south coast, it was a regular landing base for what the locals referred to as 'wetbacks': illegal immigrants swimming ashore from dodgy vessels that wouldn't chance bringing them in any closer. It was also a favourite landing place for consignments of drugs, and the town had more than its fair share of users and pushers.

The number of homeless people had also risen considerably in the last few years – many of them runaways, who often fell into stealing to feed their drug habits. Drugs had become a convenient way to blur the edges of a bleak and loveless existence. Shoplifting from supermarkets and off-licences had also risen, as had begging on the street and sleeping in shop doorways. All in all, these nomads were a pitiful and unwelcome tribe, despised by locals and shopkeepers alike, and a thorn in the side as well as the conscience of the local police.

The town also had a surrounding agricultural ring of nurseries, now steadily being bought up and built over, where casual labour was a necessity in season and these, along with the extensive building work that was rapidly expanding the place, needed workers, not all of them legal.

There was, too, a large stock of Victorian houses, mostly terraced, many seedy and rundown, where any amount of domestic and child abuse went on, rarely reported and even more rarely prosecuted. When examined closely, it was not a place anyone would choose to take an old-fashioned English seaside holiday – but then those who did visit knew nothing of these drawbacks. All they saw were the beach, the sand dunes, the amusement arcades, and the old winding streets of the town, with its easy access to the Downs and more countryside than they could shake a stick at.

DI Hardy had worked in the Littleton-on-Sea police station for longer than she cared to remember, since when it had had a minimal staff and very little to do. Now it was much expanded, with a greatly increased workforce, times had changed unrecognisably. The many departments now crammed into the building were largely insular and did not mix easily, and DI Hardy knew only a fraction of them.

She was forty-eight years old, married with two children who were hardly children anymore, and lived outside the sprawling mass that the town was becoming, in a rambling old cottage to which she was looking forward to returning on this grizzly Friday evening.

Her new DS was younger at only forty, and was also married with two children, but her life was very different, and there were no similarities at all between their domestic arrangements. Groves lived in a huge barn conversion buried in the countryside, quite a secret unless you knew where to find it, with an au pair-cum-nanny, her husband working away in the Middle East for most of the time, as he had a job in the petro-chemical industry.

Many of those working in the station considered her a rich bitch who was just passing time and slumming it, but Hardy knew better. She could see Groves was a dedicated officer who did the job to give her life purpose and direction, and counteract the smothering atmosphere of her domestic circumstances.

Both her children were away most of the time at

boarding school and, although she was comfortably off, that and her husband's habitual absence made her feel like a bird in a golden cage, with nothing to do all day except sing for release. Her job provided the necessary stuffing to fill the empty hours that filled what passed for her life.

Although they appeared outwardly so different, she and Hardy had got on rather well from the first, both giving their jobs high priority, but sharing a mutual interest in music. They both had lively minds that sometimes drove them to distraction, and they had discovered that each of them was attempting to learn how to play the flute.

Today Groves had brought her instrument into work, as her husband and children were away, and she planned to go back to the DI's house that evening for a bite to eat and an attempt at the lively jig duet that Hardy had come across. She had nothing to go home to apart from the au pair, Gerda, and she didn't really get on with the woman.

Hardy was also looking forward to this, as her husband was out on a gig tonight with his band, and she knew he would not be home until the early hours. She hoped with all her heart that this accident didn't tie them up for too long. OK, so people had died, but that was hardly her fault, and she had been looking forward keenly to having a tootle on her flute.

It was November, and thus already dark when they arrived at the site of the collision. In one car was a lone man, the one who was, even now, being cut free by the fire service. An ambulance crew stood by, awaiting his release. In the other car had been two mothers with their young daughters in the back seat. Without the restraint of seatbelts, the girls hadn't stayed there very long and, on her final fatal journey, one of them must have severed a major artery, thought Hardy, as the scene was liberally painted with a coating of blood. As Groves masked a retch with her hankie, Hardy had the irreverent thought that it was difficult to tell whether this scene represented an

11

accident in an abattoir or a modern installation art exhibit.

The deceased women had probably given in to pester power, and presumably had not insisted that their two daughters wore their seatbelts. The head-on collision had catapulted the girls forward, across the front seats, breaking their mothers' necks. They were dead, as was one of the little girls, but the other had been through the windscreen and had landed sprawled on the bonnet of the other car. She had already been conveyed to the ICU of a hospital in the larger nearby town, and the meat wagon was on its way to remove the three less fortunate travellers to the mortuary.

'God, the pity of it!' whispered Groves, her face a mask of horror.

'Should've got the little bugger to buckle up, then. There are no excuses in a situation like this,' said Hardy. She had long since hardened her heart to the consequences of such simple human errors.

'How can you be so cold?' asked Groves, staring at the DI as if she had suggested breeding children for food.

'How many adverts have there been on the telly about this sort of thing? Why don't people learn? This was an accident waiting to happen and, this time, it did. End of story.'

'I wish I could think like that.'

'If you don't learn to, you'll not last much longer in the force.'

'It's not a force now, it's a service,' said Groves to her senior officer, momentarily distracted.

'Bollocks!' Hardy replied. 'How can a service hunt down crooks, arrest them, and put them away? There's more *force* than *service* in that, when you look at it from our point of view.'

'I don't think our thoughts count anymore. It's what we are to the public.'

'More's the pity. When I was little, kids were scared

stiff of policemen. Now, they jeer at us – cock a snook at us as if we were a joke. We've had our powers so reduced that we might as well be a branch of the Mothers' Union, for all we can do about most of the little sods in this town.'

'True,' Groves mused, then pointed as a vehicle approached with lights flashing. 'Here comes Traffic. We're here out of necessity, but do you think we can just hand over to them now?'

'Watch me and weep.' Hardy approached the newly arrived car and leaned through an open window to explain the situation, withdrew her head and turned towards Groves. Her thumbs went up in the air as she wandered back over. 'All sorted. They'll make the necessary arrangements to get the road cleared, and the sergeant will go to the women's houses and break the news.

'They've already radioed through to the Drugs Squad, and asked them to attend, so I think we can leave the rest to them. Let's get back to mine and see what the old man's left us for supper.'

'Your husband cooks?'

'You bet he does. Cleans, too. He may be in a band and need to practise, but he's retired, and he's got to do something else to keep himself busy or he'd go mad – either that or I would. There are two of us grown-ups living there, and he's the one with the free time to wield the vacuum cleaner and the polishing cloth. I did it all when the kids were little and we were both working – now it's his turn. Fair's fair.'

'I'm dying to meet him,' said Groves, as if this represented a rare treat for her, 'but I don't even know his name.'

'Everybody calls him Hal, but his full name's Hallelujah Martin Luther King Hardy. How's that for a handle?'

'Good gracious! Whatever was his mother thinking of?'

'If you stay on for a bit tonight, you might meet him

13

and work that one out for yourself. Are you going to stay over?'

'I hadn't planned on it.'

'Well, I suggest you think about it. We've just witnessed a very nasty accident, and I propose to open at least one bottle of wine with supper, and the same again when we have a go at this duet. Are you on duty tomorrow?'

'No. I've just got some paperwork to catch up with.'

'I'm not due in till the evening, so I suggest you phone your au pair and tell her you won't be back. We'll nip back now and get our cars, and I expect I'll be able to hunt you out something to wear in bed, even though it'll be far too big for you.'

'Do we have to go back to the station? I won't need my car until I'm going in later in the day: it's not as if I have anything much to go home to.'

'Come on. I heard you had a fabulous barn conversion.'

'With nobody in it but the au pair, and I don't really like her if I'm being honest. We've got nothing in common, and if I do want to talk about something, she pleads a lack of understanding of English. She can speak it well enough when she chooses, though. Without the children's presence, I don't much want to spend any time there.'

'Would you like me to drop you off when I go in late tomorrow afternoon?'

'Thank you very much,' replied Groves gratefully. She'd worked in a station further along the coast before she was transferred to Littleton-on-Sea and moved house, and she didn't have many friends locally. She and Hardy had worked their first case together very politely and formally, but the recent realisation that both of them were enthusiastic novice flautists had sparked off a warmth in their relationship, and made them sisters in arms against the mysteries of those shiny metal tubes with all the little holes.

'And I think you could call me Olivia when we're not in the office, especially if we're going to be socialising together over supper.'

'Thanks ... Olivia. Then you'd better call me Lauren. I am looking forward to this duet.'

'Me too. Hey, do you know what I heard that little rat Redwood doing the other day when he thought we couldn't hear?'

'No. I never heard anything derogatory.'

'I heard him whistling the theme tune from the Laurel and Hardy films under his breath.'

'Why?'

'Have you ever thought about what we look like side by side? And if you examine our names, you're Lauren – not quite Laurel – and I'm Hardy. Ha ha, very funny. The next time Traffic's short of a body, he can go along and help out, and I hope it's on a freezing cold day with driving rain and sleet.'

'Blasted cheek of the man!'

Olivia Hardy turned the car in the direction of her home and mused on the surprising things that could turn a professional partnership into a friendship. In their case, it looked like the flute might prove to be the catalyst, and she felt it would be nice to have a decent relationship with her working partner. Her previous one had been nearing retirement and taciturn to the point of almost complete silence. She had never got to know him, having found their working life together very barren and lonely.

It had not been possible to form any sort of friendship with other officers at the station because of a lack of compatible senior ranks. Often abrupt, she knew she could appear aloof at times, not willing to settle for the shallow matiness that her male colleagues seemed to accept – more a cult of the penis than a recognition of ability, she felt. A DS, though, would be considered suitable as a friend as well as colleague, especially as they were both women.

After about ten minutes, she pulled off the main road on to a small side road and, after four hundred yards, turned right on to a narrow driveway. 'This is it,' she said, braking at the front of a long, low thatched property with leaded lights.

'Oh, how pretty!' exclaimed Lauren, climbing out of the car to have a closer look. 'It looks like you even have roses round the door in the summer. How long have you lived here?'

'Almost all our married lives. Hal's parents didn't want to sell it, but they did want to retire from the NHS and go back home. We live here for now, and if they come back, they'll live here again. If they don't, well, it's here when they drop off their perches. We'll sort something out if and when the situation arises.'

It seemed odd, disclosing this sort of personal information to a colleague, but as she intended to extract some personal details from the DS, it seemed only fair. It would certainly be nice to have a friend in her work colleague, as there weren't many people comfortable about a friendship with a member of the police force – damn, *service* – whoever they were. There was always that slight discomfort there that they had to be on their best behaviour all the time. She, too, was looking forward to having a partner in her wrestle with that difficult instrument, and tonight would be the highlight of her week.

As they entered the cottage, Lauren exclaimed with pleasure, 'This is absolutely charming. You must be very happy here.'

'We are, for now. Now, let's see what Hal's left us for supper.'

Hal had left them a pot of spicy lamb stew and a pot of rice to be heated in the microwave, so it wasn't long before they sat down to eat, with the first of the glasses of wine they would consume that evening.

When they had cleared away the plates and opened another bottle of chilled Sauvignon Blanc, Olivia got out the two copies of the duet she had found and asked Lauren if she would be able to play her part through on the upright piano which nestled against the far wall of the small dining room, never giving a thought to whether she would be capable of doing so.

'No problem. Lead me to it,' she replied enthusiastically, and Olivia smiled as she realised that her colleague was beginning to relax under the benign influence of the wine, and certainly could handle going through her part on the old Joanna. They stood in front of the instrument with a copy of the jig on the hanging music stand, and made a good fist of playing it through at a fair lick, Olivia taking the top part, Lauren the lower one.

'I don't think I can go that fast on the flute,' admitted Lauren.

'Me neither,' replied her boss, with a heartfelt sigh of relief. 'What part do you want to play on the flute?'

'Can I take the lower part? Only I've noticed a couple of high Ds in the top part, and I can't blow them yet.'

'Well, I can just about manage that. How are you in the middle register?'

'A bit shaky. I don't really seem to have the confidence.'

'Well, I'll open another bottle of wine, and we'll extract such Dutch courage as we can from that.'

Lauren had brought her flute in with her, opened the case and began to fit it together. 'I'll just get mine,' her hostess said, and went into another room, coming out with her instrument already put together. 'Well,' she said, 'I can't always be bothered to put it away when I've finished with it.'

'I wouldn't dare leave mine out. That interfering, nosy au pair would no doubt have a go at playing it, and she'd probably break it, then deny all knowledge of what had happened.'

'Here's to making sweet music together,' said Olivia, handing her sergeant another full glass, and they toasted each other and music in general, before both taking a goodly swallow. Music stands had appeared from nowhere, and as they settled down, the DI announced, 'It's in 6/8 time. I come in first, so it's me after five, then you join in.'

They played through the piece very slowly, inaccurately, and with lots of minuscule breaks for swearing. 'The only time I use bad language is when I'm sight-reading music,' confessed Lauren, and Olivia knew exactly what she meant.

After a couple more attempts, trying to increase the tempo each time, they were both helpless with laughter, and Olivia refilled their glasses. 'And now for the best bit: I set my little sound-activated tape recorder on the table, so we can listen to ourselves from a more critical position.'

'You've what?'

'You'll find it funny. I used to do this with an old schoolfriend with piano duets, and we used to laugh until we cried when we heard what we were actually like. Keep an open mind.'

When the front door opened later to admit Hal, they were both helpless with mirth, and didn't even notice his arrival until he spoke.

'What's tickling you two ladies' funny bones?'

Lauren reacted with shock, whipping round her head to look at the large black man who filled the small doorway from the hall. 'Who ...?' she cried, only to be cut off by her inspector.

'Hello, Hal. This is Lauren, my DS. We were just sight-reading a flute duet, and I recorded our efforts. We've just listened to the tape and it was hilarious.'

'Can I have a listen, too?'

'Course you can,' replied his wife, and played the

recording for a second time.

Hal was suitably amused, and was finally formally introduced to Lauren. 'Hal's a musician,' Olivia explained, thinking this might go part of the way to explaining why he was in a brightly coloured shirt covered in images of parrots.

'What do you play?' asked Lauren, still confused.

'The steel drums. I'm originally from Barbados. I used to be a teacher, but I took early retirement and now I just do what I love best, which is playing in steel bands all over this part of the coast.'

Lauren was thunderstruck. She'd never imagined such an interesting and exotic husband for her outwardly conventional boss: no suited businessman for the inspector but this gaudy peacock of a man. Lauren realised she had led a sheltered life, and had grown up in a protective Middle England bubble which had shaped her expectations of others.

'If you want to come upstairs, I'll show you my kit, after I've lugged it back up there. Give me about half an hour, and I'll have a glass of that wine, too, honey. Entertaining's a thirsty business.'

His wife poured him a generous glassful, which he downed like it were water, then went to open yet another bottle. 'You didn't think you'd get an early night, did you?' she asked her new friend. 'Once he's shown you his kit and let you have a go, he'll want us to play the duet again so that he can busk a piano accompaniment to it.'

'I had no idea you were so interested in music.'

'What good would spreading that abroad do in our job? Someone would only find a way to ridicule my interest, and they've got enough to work with, with my rotund figure and my ... *casual* dress sense – not to mention my name.'

'You don't sound very bitter about it,' said Lauren, bemused by the DI's relaxed attitude.

'While they're having a go at me, they're leaving somebody else alone. I've got the skin of an elephant as well as the figure to go along with it. What they don't know is that I also have the memory of one, and I'll get my own back at some unspecified time in the future. I'm just biding my time for now.'

A loud holler from upstairs interrupted their discussion, and Olivia led Lauren upstairs to play with her husband's second-favourite toys.

After half an hour of drum demonstrations, and a quasi-lecture about how the instrument had evolved and attempts at playing the drums herself, Hal finally bellowed, 'Where's that bottle of wine? And is there any of that stew left? Me stomach thinks me throat's cut. Chop chop, woman. You're starving your husband to death, not to mention giving him a bad case of lack of booze.'

The three of them went back downstairs, glasses were filled, and Hal served himself a plateful of the remains of the supper, eating it standing up without bothering to reheat it. As he ate, he began to tell Lauren about his parents, and why they'd left the cottage.

'They were both dentists, working on the NHS and privately. They bought this place when they were first working here and it was in a bad state of repair. Gradually they renovated it, and when it was finally finished, the opportunity arose for them to retire.

'They moved back to Barbados. That was years ago – I'm an only child – and they seem to be quite happily settled there. I can't really see them coming back, but we're keeping the home fires burning in case they have a sudden urge to move back to the grey and rainy climes of Britain.'

'Fat chance of that happening,' his wife commented, heading towards the kitchen with a corkscrew in her hand, her gait a little unsteady.

As she returned with yet another bottle of wine, Lauren

asked a little tentatively, 'I don't see any signs of your children. I understood you had two.'

Olivia sighed deeply as she filled their glasses again. 'We do. Hibbie decided to leave school, much to our disappointment as we wanted her to go on to university. She's now doing a course at college, an admin qualification, and has a job a little further along the coast. Benjamin has just started at college. We just didn't go into their rooms when we were upstairs and, to be honest, they're hardly ever at home these days. They're sixteen and eighteen, by the way, Ben's the elder.'

'What's Hibbie short for?' asked the sergeant, not being able to unravel the source of the diminutive in her slightly befuddled state.

'Hibiscus Flower. Don't look at me. It's was his mother's idea, not mine.'

Hal smiled at this comment, and his booming laugh filled the room. 'If we hadn't named our daughter after her suggestion there would have been hell to pay, and we didn't want to name her after her grandmother. My mother's given name is Morning Glory, known to everyone just as Glory.'

'Oh.' Lauren couldn't think of any other comment to make. 'Mine are Jade and Sholto – eight and ten – kids, that is. I do miss them when they're away at school. This is Jade's first term, so the house is very empty without her.'

'Do they have to go away to school?' asked Hal, who found the practice of sending small children away to boarding schools barbaric.

'It's the only way to get them a decent start in life these days,' replied Lauren, then began to bluster. 'Not that I mean … not with yours … I'm sure they had a perfectly good …' She finally stuttered to a stop.

'That's OK, Lauren,' declared Olivia, 'I wouldn't exactly say that ours have turned out as model young citizens. Sometimes I wish we'd had the money to send them somewhere decent, even if they were only day pupils.'

Hal growled deep in the back of his throat in disapproval – he had been a state school teacher before he retired – before grabbing the neck of the bottle for a little top-up. A swig soon restored his goodwill, and he asked Lauren what she did when she wasn't working.

'I don't do all that much, to be quite honest, what with Kenneth working away so much.'

'You must do something,' he persisted. 'Lord, I'm still hungry.'

As he went in search of the cake tin, Lauren shrugged and explained that her only interests were music and needlework, and she was lonely a lot of the time.

'Well, if we're off duty together, you've got a musical partner now.'

'That's true. I don't suppose you play recorder, do you?'

'Of course I do. I have a whole family of different sizes put away in a cupboard. Do you want to do that next time?

'Next time?'

'Of course. We're a musical partnership now. If you want to be, that is,' said Olivia, slightly unsure of herself in making this assumption.

'I'd love to do that. We'll have to compare rosters.' Lauren was definitely getting bleary-eyed now, and put her head back, allowing her eyes to close.

When Hal came back with a huge wedge of cake in one hand, his jaws working away on this second supper, Olivia pointed at her and said, 'I think you ought to help her up to her room. We had a call out to a filthy accident just before we went off duty, but I think she's relaxed enough now not to have nightmares.'

Hal gathered the tall, unresisting figure, which was just beginning to emit small, polite snores, up into his arms and headed for the staircase. 'I'll be back in a minute, and you can tell me about that accident. I know that if you don't get it off your chest you'll have nightmares yourself.'

CHAPTER TWO

The next morning didn't start until 10.30 for any of them, when there were three pairs of bleary eyes at the breakfast table, and three jaded palates trying to enjoy the home-made marmalade spread liberally on their toast.

'Do you think you could drop me home for a change of clothes before we go into the station?' asked Lauren, anxiously hoping that she wasn't being a nuisance – but she had after all slept in what she was wearing, with just a duvet put over her comatose body.

'No problem,' replied Olivia. 'It'll give me a chance to have a quick peek at where you live.'

'Of course. I'll give you the guided tour, and just hope we don't run into Gerda – she's the au pair I don't particularly get on with. Maybe she'll be out shopping, or whatever it is she does most of the time now there are no children to look after.'

'Great! I love looking at other people's houses, although some of the ones we visit in our job aren't exactly of the ideal home variety, are they?'

After several cups of coffee and a couple of painkillers, Olivia declared herself safe to drive, and they bade goodbye to Hal for a short while. Before they drove off in the pool car, they could hear the sounds of the Caribbean coming from the room upstairs where his set of steel drums lived in the winter. Apparently, in the summer, he relocated them to an old barn at the back of the property, so that his practice wasn't too much of a disturbance in the house.

Home Farm Barn was a couple of miles to the west and

further inland, proving to be a substantial building that had been renovated beyond recognition and now represented a very up-market dwelling. There was a huge double-height entrance lobby with sofas and a central table with a large vase of flowers on its highly polished centre.

Every room was on a grand scale, and a single staircase right in the middle of the vestibule split halfway up, and led in opposite directions to the bedrooms. 'Bloody hell! You didn't let on it was this grand, and so off the beaten track,' exclaimed Olivia in disbelief.

'Kenneth has a very high salary,' was the only explanation she got, and this was said apologetically.

In Lauren's bedroom, Olivia, having no regard for other people's privacy, flung back all the wardrobe doors in what appeared to be a dressing room. 'Bloody hell,' she carolled, again. 'You've got enough suits in here to start your own company!' A whole row of navy, grey, and black suits and pale blouses hung neatly on parade. Another set of doors revealed some very expensive day wear, and yet another, a row of what looked like ball gowns. 'Very fancy,' she commented drily.

'We used to go to a lot of social events when Kenneth was working in Scotland,' Lauren explained, half-apologetically. The children's bedrooms were like those on TV adverts, and the spare rooms were also immaculate. In silence, they headed back downstairs.

'What's through here?' asked the inspector, indicating what looked like another front door that led off a very spacious utility room.

Lauren sighed and muttered, 'That's the granny annexe which Kenneth decided we needed for when his mother comes to live with us.' Her face was a mask of inscrutability, and Olivia couldn't help herself.

'You don't look as if that's something you want to happen anytime soon.'

'Well ... I don't want it to happen. Ever. To be honest,

I want things to be like they were, when the children attended the small local school, and we didn't have Gerda around all the time.'

'No chance of that, I suppose?'

'None whatsoever. Kenneth wouldn't countenance the children going to the local comprehensive, and Gerda cleans and cooks as well as babysitting. He said that as long as I work, then we need her – and that his mother has bad arthritis, and will need somewhere small and self-contained with help at hand should she need it.'

'Where does Gerda sleep?'

'In a small apartment in the attic area.'

'Lock her in. I dare you.' Olivia was feeling defensive of her new friend, and felt that she really had on golden handcuffs. If she gave up work, she'd still have to live here, and her mother-in-law would no doubt be installed sooner than she would, if the mistress – supposed – of the house was working full-time.

As the inspector looked about her, not in envy but with the thought that she preferred her own homely cottage, Lauren spoke again. 'Thank you so much for last night. I don't know when I've had more fun. Can we do it again in the not too distant future?'

'If you're really good, I'll take you to one of Hal's band's gigs.' Woah! She didn't want to become haunted by her sergeant, although Lauren would be welcome as a friend. And it had been fun to play the flute with someone about as inept as she was. F sharps and B flats were best described with the full swear words in front of them, the way they had played the night before.

That said, she did love playing the recorder, and had just been treated to an alto sax for her birthday by Hal, in the hope that, one day, she might play with the band. She wondered if Lauren would agree to get herself a sax, so that they could learn together. It really helped, in their job, to have something that totally engaged and saturated the mind, and took it off all the desperate scenes they had to view.

'Come back to ours for lunch,' she offered. 'I've got a proposition I want to put to you.'

'That sounds very mysterious.'

'Just wait till we get back. There's something I want to ask you that you may find interesting.'

Lauren had instantly agreed to purchase a saxophone. It was something she had thought about, in a vague sort of way, now and again, but this gave her a solid excuse to buy one, and the thought of having someone to learn with was great. This 'instant' friendship had brought home to her just how lonely she was when she wasn't on duty.

They took the ring road to the office, and Olivia had a bright flash of memory back to when the only way through the town was via a swing bridge over the river. The building of this alternative route had been a blessing, but one that was now no longer valued as it had been, due to the monstrous sprawl of housing that spread across what had been agricultural land to the north, all the way to the downs.

The road was now very busy with all the extra traffic, and often completely blocked, as it was now. They sat in the queue, looking around them for some sort of diversion. A single field which a local grower had refused to give up drew Lauren's attention, and she pointed out the lone figure in the middle of it. 'That's a bit of a tatterdemalion tattybogle, don't you think?' she asked.

'A *what*?' queried Olivia. 'I can tell you've lived in Scotland.'

'Sorry. A very tatty scarecrow.'

'A scarecrow? At this time of year?' said Olivia, looking in the direction that Lauren was. Suddenly she braked and stopped the car, manoeuvring it into the gateway to the field and out of the barely moving flow of traffic. 'What are you doing?' queried her passenger.

'That scarecrow's moving, if my eyesight doesn't deceive me.'

Lauren squinted into the distance. 'Are you sure it's not just the clothes being blown by the wind?' she asked.

'The clothes seem to be bound to the body. Come on. We're going to take a look,' decided Olivia, getting swiftly out of the car and opening the gate.

She was right, and as they neared the figure, they could see that it was, in fact, human, and was making weak movements to try to draw attention to itself. 'Good God! Who on earth would do a vile thing like that?'

When they reached the figure, they could discern that it was, or had been, a youth. His eyes were blacked and swollen, there was the imprint of the toe-cap of a boot on his forehead, his nose was broken, and he had some teeth missing.

'It looks like he's taken a hell of a beating,' Hardy said. 'Phone for assistance as quickly as you can. Oh, and from now on, we'd better not use first names. Back to Sergeant, and Inspector or ma'am.

'Ambulance on its way, CSI team being scrambled, ma'am,' replied the DS in her most formal tone.

'CSI? What happened to SOCO teams?'

'Gone. Swept away in the rush for keeping up with the times, I suppose.'

'Bugger. Can't they leave anything alone? It's going to be all right, son,' she finished softly, putting up a hand to the figure bound on the cross of wooden poles. 'Sergeant, go to the car and look in the boot. There should be a tool kit in there, and maybe you can find a pair of pliers to get rid of some of these wires. The blood supply to his hands is all but cut off.'

Groves scurried across the field to search for the tool, but before she had returned, they could hear the siren of an approaching ambulance. The station wasn't far away, and they were arriving in double-quick time. Arriving back at the inspector's side, the DS handed over the pliers, as the ambulance was trying to park, and Hardy began to cut the wires restricting the circulation in the lad's hands, but as soon as she started, he began to scream in a high-pitched voice.

'You'd better leave it to the professionals, ma'am. You could do more harm than good if you don't know what you're doing.'

'I'm only trying to help,' snapped Hardy, her voice harsh as she registered the distress in the young man's yells, and her legs turning to jelly.

'Well, it doesn't seem to be working that way, does it, guv?' replied Groves with immaculate logic.

'You're right. Sorry, son. The ambulance has just arrived and they'll get you down and into hospital in just a few moments.'

The wailing continued unabated, and both women had the almost irresistible urge to put their fingers in their ears to block out the obscenity of human suffering, but both realised that they should be talking to this poor soul who had been so ill-used.

'Keep calm and don't try to free yourself. You'll likely do more damage than good. The paramedics will be here in just a couple of minutes.' Hardy had to almost shout to be heard through the howls and screams, but she tried to make her voice comforting and confident.

'You'll be nice and comfortable in a hospital bed before you know it,' called Groves, but their words could do nothing to penetrate the agony of the figure hanging there looking like a crucified criminal.

When the paramedics made it to the scene, one of the first things they did was to give him something to relieve the pain, then talked to him as they worked at the wires fixing him in position. He continued to wail for quite a while, as it was a tricky operation, untangling the mess of wire that had been used to bind him, and Lauren had to absent herself for a few minutes to throw up behind a bush.

Once as much painkiller as was safe to use had finally been administered, his screams died down to a pathetic whimpering. Groves returned wiping her mouth with a cotton handkerchief and apologised for her momentary lapse.

'Don't worry about it,' answered Hardy. 'I nearly followed you over and did exactly the same. I can't abide the sound of someone in agony, and that was harrowing. I'm sure we were very lucky not to be on the other end of it.'

As the medical staff gently lowered him on to the stretcher, he gave an almighty scream, and the two women winced, Groves giving another dry heave as her stomach rebelled again.

'Let us know how he is, won't you?' Hardy requested, glad that they were not going in the ambulance with him. She felt harrowed almost beyond endurance. She had come across great suffering in her professional life, usually at the scenes of accidents, but she had encountered nothing like this before in all her years in the force, or rather, service.

They waited for the arrival of the CSI team and after some discussion left the field.

'Just drop me in the car park,' said Groves in a voice made husky with stomach acid. 'The paperwork can wait. I just don't feel up to talking about this. I just want to go home.'

'Fair enough. I wish I could do the same, but it's Saturday night, and anything could happen. You know what the seafront clubs are like at the weekend.'

'Rather you than me.'

'You realise what we've just witnessed, don't you?'

'Enlighten me.'

'The first potential murder case working together.'

'Don't say that. He's not dead yet.'

'I'd put money on it.' DI Hardy wasn't one of life's optimists. 'All the same, I had better get an officer dispatched to sit with him in case he is lucid enough to talk.'

Maybe it was the cold, miserable weather, or the sleety rain that started about nine o'clock, but it was very quiet for a Saturday, and DI Hardy was able to get through some of her reports and figures with barely an interruption.

She got home just before midnight, only preceding Hal by about ten minutes. As he came through the front door, she looked up from the book she was trying to concentrate on and asked, 'Close early, did they?'

'There was nothing doing. I think you ought to get someone in plain clothes in there next Saturday night, though. There seemed to be some under-the-counter business going on at the bar that I think might interest your lot. Mmm, you smell nice,' he concluded, dropping a kiss on the top of her head.

'New shampoo. Had to shower as soon as I got in. I got rather bloodied earlier in the day, and had to get out of my clothes before I puked. Drugs?'

'I reckon so. The regular barman wasn't in, and his replacement seemed to have other business on his mind rather than that of serving drinks. Just a word to the wise, that's all.'

'I'll sort it out when I'm in next. Thanks for the heads-up.'

While Hal was lugging in his instruments, Olivia was surprised to find her mobile phone ringing, and answered it to find Lauren on the other end of the call. She was sobbing into the handset, sounding as if her heart was breaking. 'Whatever is it, Lauren?' asked the inspector, wondering if there had been some tragedy in her personal life.

'It's just that lad we found. I can still hear him screaming. What am I going to do? I can't get it out of my mind.'

'Look, I wasn't going to tell you till tomorrow, but he didn't make it. He slipped away in the ambulance, but you can comfort yourself that he didn't die out in that field, and at least we made sure that his pain was dulled, and that he was warm and as comfortable as he could be when he went.'

'Can I sleep at yours tonight?' the younger woman asked, unexpectedly.

'Er, well, I suppose so ... and I've got some sleeping tablets that you can take, but, Lauren, you've got to grow a thicker skin. I have to ask ... how did you make sergeant, if this sort of thing upsets you so much?'

She didn't want to have to nanny her sergeant. Lauren was a grown woman, a wife and mother, and theirs was supposed to be a grown-up relationship, forged through the adversity of being in the same profession. On the other hand, she didn't have a husband to go home to, and her children were away at school, whereas her own husband had just arrived back and her children were still around, although currently on the AWOL list.

'I haven't the faintest idea, but I've never seen or heard anything like today before in all my time in the police. Can I come now, please?'

'Come on over. Company will do you good, and with one of my little bombs inside you, you'll sleep like a top.'

'Thanks, ma'am ... Olivia. I'm on my way.'

When she got to the cottage, there was no peace to be had there, though. She could hear the shouting from outside the front door.

'You bloody stupid thoughtless little shit. How could you do this to me in my position? You could lose me my job, as well as frying your own brain,' she heard, before

Hal opened the door to her stentorian knock.

'Do you want to end up in the gutter or in a filthy squat with a dirty needle in your arm?'

'I only took a bit of blow,' replied a voice Lauren had not heard before.

'Ben,' said Hal in explanation. 'I saw him in the club, although he was too drunk to notice I was there. It would seem that he's now experimenting with drugs, and Olivia's not too pleased.'

'I thought he was at college,' she almost whispered as he beckoned her to come inside.

'It's the local college, and he just goes in every day, but not usually from here. He stays at mates' houses so much that he might as well not live here. Tonight he's decided to show his face, but apart from his mother knowing all the signs, he doesn't know yet that I saw him buying something from under the bar at the club.'

'Should I go?'

'Not at all. Let them yell themselves out, and we'll sit in the kitchen with a glass of wine. I'll go through when things aren't quite so heated and read him the riot act in fairly calm tones, pointing out that he's taken his first step on the road to hell. It might do some good, and at least it'll get Olivia off her high horse for now. What a stupid little shit he's been, though.'

'Look, Olivia said something about sleeping tablets. If I could just have one of those, I'll go back home. You don't need me here tonight. It's been a tough day, and you've got this to cope with on top of what happened earlier.'

'Give me a minute, and I'll see if she's got some in the downstairs bathroom.' Hal returned a couple of minutes later with a small wrap of tissue paper in his right hand. 'I've put two in, just in case. Are you sure you don't want to stay on?'

'I'm sure. I'm a big girl now, and it's time I started acting like one. Thank Olivia for saying I could come over, but I need to face up to this on my own, because that's how I usually have to cope with everything else … on my own.'

When Hal went into the sitting room to take over the lecture from his wife, Olivia was surprised but ultimately relieved to find that Lauren had already left. Another bird with a broken wing was the last thing on her list of things she wanted, at the moment.

Ben mixed up in drugs was one of her recurring nightmares and, come to think of it, she hadn't seen Hibbie for some days. She worked in the next town, and, as she had a friend there who hadn't left school yet, she'd asked if she could stay with her for the half-term break. Now Olivia came to think of it, it wasn't half term. That had passed, and she'd just been too busy at work to take that fact in. What was the little madam up to? She'd have to phone the friend and find out exactly what was going on, and when Hibbie came back, have a stern talk about keeping her word when parental trust was put in her. Her daughter had been given a freedom that many others of her age were not, and Olivia was determined she should live up to it.

CHAPTER THREE

'He had no ID on him – nothing in his pockets, no wallet, no phone, nothing. We've got no idea who he is, and his clothes are just washed-out cheap brands that he could've bought new or even in a jumble sale. We don't even know what he looks like, he was so badly beaten. We need to find out who this poor kid was and who did this to him.

'Start with missing persons, and check his fingerprints and DNA against the national database. Put out a message on the local radio that we've found a young lad, murdered, about eighteen or nineteen. Give them a description and ask for anyone with information to come forward. Also, go round the local squats and the homeless and see if any one of their number is missing. This poor lad didn't just drop out of the sky.

'I'll see if I can get someone to try to build a photofit of him looking something like he must have looked before he took that savage beating, and I'll get copies to all of you to use on your travels. Good luck.'

Thus DI Hardy addressed her troops the following morning. Singling out Colin Redwood to try the squats and the shop doorways, she went off to bag herself someone who could do the photofit picture, with the DC's whining following her down the corridor.

'I know it's cold outside, Colin, and some of the squatters and homeless aren't very polite people, but you're a copper. If it makes you feel better, take one of the Uniforms with you in case you need nannying.' All this was called over her shoulder, as Redwood did his usual name-calling and one-fingered salute just out of her eyeline.

He seemed too thick to realise that as long as he kept doing that sort of thing, he was going to get all the shitty jobs. She really didn't see him going far in CID, and could easily see him back in uniform before long if he didn't pull up his socks and show some respect for rank.

The word 'nanny' had brought thoughts of her DS to her mind, but she immediately dismissed them. Lauren wasn't on duty today, and she should be all right at home. There really was no need to phone her and see how she was. With a shake of her head, she carried on looking for someone competent enough to fashion a likeness of their dead lad from post-mortem photographs. She'd have to chase up when the post-mortem was going to be, too. Their regular Forensic Medical Examiner was away for the weekend, so she'd probably have to wait until tomorrow for that to happen.

Once again it was a quiet shift, and she managed to complete all her reports for the end of the previous month. Hardy was a stickler when it came to getting the crime figures in on time, and simply wouldn't tolerate tardiness in this respect. If the lower-ranked officers didn't comply, the complaints came down from above, a direct line from Superintendent Devenish, and landed on her. The buck stopped at her desk, and she was well aware of this. Why should she get a bollocking because the other ranks were too lazy or too derelict in their duty to get them to her on time?

By lunchtime she had as much of a likeness as she was likely to get of the dead youth, and she diligently issued a couple of copies to each officer as they came back for lunch. 'Use these this afternoon, and don't come back till you've got me a name,' she told them all. 'We need to identify who he was before we can contemplate looking for who did this to him, and why.'

By the end of her shift, they still had no name, but not

every place had yet been tried, and there were probably a couple of squats they didn't even know about. Advising them to try snouts and known dealers next, just on the off-chance that the lad had been involved with drugs, Olivia put on her coat to go home, realising that she had been glad Lauren wasn't on duty today.

Olivia had dressed particularly scruffily for the day, in jogging bottoms and an old sweatshirt, and she feared that her sergeant's always-immaculate dress sense was going to force her to examine the clothes she regularly wore into work, and probably smarten herself up a bit. She could do with it – had even been spoken to from on high about it – but had resisted so far for the sake of comfort. Dammit, her sergeant was going to do what the approbation of a senior officer couldn't achieve: stir her conscience about the impression she gave to members of the public. She went home that night in a thoughtful frame of mind.

When Hal got in from a rehearsal in a buddy's garage, he found her turfing out her clothes cupboards and drawers. 'What the hell are you doing, woman?' he asked.

'Throwing out the worst of my clothes. I desperately need some new stuff for work.'

'What's brought all this on, huh?'

'Nothing. I just think that, at my rank, I should make a smarter impression on the members of the public that I have to deal with.'

'Smart? You? The world's gone mad,' he concluded, going back downstairs to raid the fridge.

On Monday morning, DI Hardy surprised the whole station by turning up in a respectable skirt and blazer over a white blouse, and Teri Friend, who she passed in the hallway, asked her if she had an extra-marital date after work.

'Shut your cheeky mouth,' she responded, without turning round to see Teri break out into a large grin. One-nil, Olivia thought, as she answered the phone.

When Lauren got in she looked at the inspector in silent amazement, but tried so hard not to say anything that she went red in the face. Olivia looked at her and commented, 'There's no need to say it, OK? I just decided that I ought to make a bit more effort, that's all.'

Lauren sat down at her desk and turned on her computer to check for any new emails. 'How's your son?' she asked, tentatively, hoping that she wasn't risking a bawling-out for this personal question in the office.

'Suitably chastened, I hope, but he's eighteen now. What can we realistically do? If he carries on the way he's been going, our only options are to either shop him or chuck him out, and neither of those would end happily.'

'See if he settles down for a bit – and if he doesn't, why don't you take him over to the rehabilitation centre and show him the state some of the addicts get into?'

'That's a damned good idea. I'll leave things be for now, but the slightest hint that he's been near drugs again and I'll drag him over there – kicking and screaming if I have to. This is not a good town for kids of his age, as we discovered the other day.'

As she calmed down, Hardy's phone rang and she answered it to find DC Redwood on the other end. 'We need help here,' he gasped. 'Probably the fire service, and if they can't do anything, we'll definitely need an ambulance to scrape this bloke off the ground.'

'Slow down and tell me exactly what's happening,' responded Hardy, anxious for details of what had so upset her normally unflappable young pup of a DC.

'There's a bloke on the roof, and he's threatening to jump,' came down the line at her.

'What bloke? What roof? Why is he threatening to jump? Calm down and tell me slowly, Colin.'

'I'm outside a squat in River Road – one of those tall, thin old houses. I came here with a Uniform and we went inside. There was this bloke using a bong, and he thought we were either going to arrest him on a drugs charge, or throw him out on to the street. There was no reasoning with him, and he went straight up to the attic and got up on to the roof. I've come outside to keep an eye on him, but the Uniform's gone up to the skylight to try to talk some sense into him.'

'First piece of advice, don't panic. You'll panic *him*. What sort of state is he in?'

'Paranoid, I'd say.'

'Who's the PC?'

'It's not a PC. Sergeant Sutcliffe was the only officer available, and she volunteered to come with me.'

'Is she talking to him?'

'Yes.'

'Then you should be all right. Go back in, go upstairs and see how she's getting on, but stay on the line.'

Hardy waited about two minutes, then Colin's voice sounded again in her ear. 'Sergeant Sutcliffe says he's ready to come down, but he's frozen with fear and can't move. Thing is, some of the tiles aren't that secure, and he's already sent a couple smashing to the ground. He's getting panicky now, about falling.'

'Penny Sutcliffe will talk him down. Tell her I've just alerted the fire service, and they're on their way with a ladder, if she can't do anything with him.'

Cutting the call short, she did as she had promised, and awaited results with interest. Colin Redwood could be a cocky little sod, but this incident had unnerved him – probably the thought of blood and guts on the ground right at his feet.

Dismissing it from her mind, she was surprised to see Redwood re-enter the office a couple of hours later looking very green around the gills. 'What happened?' she asked, wondering where he had been for so long.

'Tiles slipped,' he stated curtly, slumping into his chair.

'And?'

'The bloke slipped off. 'Scuse me.' He rushed from the office towards the gents and returned ten minutes later looking pasty and strained. 'Sorry about that. It wasn't pretty.'

'You sit down again and I'll get you a nice cup of tea,' Groves volunteered, coming over all maternal at the young man's evident distress.

Ignoring this act of kindness, Hardy asked him brusquely if he'd got anywhere with tracing who the previous dead youth may have been.

'Nothing, guv,' he replied. 'Nobody's ever seen him before in their lives. It's as if he appeared out of nowhere, with no friends and no family to identify him.'

'Bollocks! He must have lived somewhere, and he needed money to live. This afternoon you can try the job centre, the benefits office, and the post offices. Somebody somewhere knows who he is, and we need to find them. Get that tea down your neck, and get back out there. You can write up your notes later.'

'You're all sweetness and light, guv.' Redwood was obviously beginning to feel a little better. As he finished his tea, Penny Sutcliffe entered the CID office and went straight to the young DC's desk.

'How are you feeling now, Colin? A bit better? Ghastly things happen when you're in this job, and you just have to absorb them and file them away. Don't dwell on what we saw, just deal with it.' She patted him on the back and went over to Hardy's desk to have a word.

Leaning over to speak in a low voice that would not carry round the entire office, she said, 'Go easy on him for the moment. It was pretty vile. He was very shaken up.'

'I take your point, Penny, but he's got to get back on the horse. I can't let him mope around in the office dwelling on it. He's got to get straight back out there and get on with the job. I've got an unidentified dead lad and I need a name for him, even if it's just to let his next of kin know what's happened to him.'

'Just use kid gloves. He's only twenty-two.'

'At twenty-two I was in Traffic and scraping boy racers off the roads round here. He's got to toughen up a bit or he'll be no use to me.'

'Just cut him some slack for the rest of today,' concluded Sutcliffe, turning to leave the office.

Looking up, Hardy called to Groves, 'Do you know where the homeless hang out during the day?'

'I know quite a few of their haunts,' replied the DS.

'Can you take Colin with you and go round them with that photofit? I'd feel happier if there were two of you. You never know what one of them will be capable of if he – or she's – off their heads on some street muck.'

'Will do, guv,' replied Groves, and walked over to Colin Redwood's desk, almost maternally, as if collecting him from school.

After they had left, the inspector received a phone call from Dr Dylan MacArthur, the FME who had returned to work after his weekend away. 'That's a fine couple of bloody messes, literally, that you've landed me in after a nice weekend in the country with my friends.'

'It's hardly my fault if someone gets offed and another lunatic threatens to throw himself off a roof.'

'Granted. Now, as to your first body …' Hardy could see him now on the other end of the phone, with his mass of just-beginning-to-grey curls, his strangely flecked cat-like green eyes and the bow tie he habitually wore, 'there was a whole mess of drugs in his bloodstream.

'He'd had the shit kicked out of him, then was strung up. His system just couldn't take anymore, and he died from a haemorrhaging ruptured spleen. It must have bled out slowly, then had a bit of a gush, probably from when he was taken down from that thing that was in the notes. It couldn't have been foreseen or avoided. The poor lad was done for from the moment that whoever it was put the boot in.

'Now, your other body, or what's left of it, was a simple fall, although there's nothing simple about falling from one of those tall houses. Blood loss from massive trauma. Any idea who these kids were?'

'Not yet, but I've got a young PC, Liam Shuttleworth, going round there to see if anyone else has returned to the address. He's a rugby player, and built like a brick shithouse, so he'll take no nonsense from any complaining squatters.'

'Keep me informed, just for the sake of interest.'

When Shuttleworth returned, he hadn't turned up a name as such, only a nickname: Shifty. He did have a rather dog-eared photograph, which had been lent to him by a grubby girl with dirty blonde dreadlocks who claimed to have been Shifty's girlfriend. 'I also brought back an old library book that she had claimed was his, so that we could run his fingerprints through the system.'

'Well done, Shuttleworth. You'll go far. You've even thought to put the book in an evidence bag. Off you go with it, then. No time to lose.' Shuttleworth shambled off.

By the end of the shift, the fingerprints of the man who had slipped from the roof had been identified as those of a local petty crook who'd been in trouble with the police since he was a child, but he was into nothing big-time, and it just seemed a tragic waste that he had lost his life while high on illegal drugs. At least they had a contact for next of kin now, though, and the case could be wrapped up quickly and efficiently: but there was still no luck with a name for the lad in the field.

Just as she was leaving, Hardy saw Groves and Redwood enter the building, but they shook their heads at her. They must have drawn a blank with their photofit: either that, or the homeless had closed ranks on them.

When she got home, Hal wasn't in, but she could smell

smoke, and there was a rule that there was no smoking inside the cottage. And it wasn't just tobacco smoke, either. This was rather more exotic. With a bellow of rage she charged up the stairs to her son's room, and found him sitting on his bed with a very benign expression on his face.

'What the bloody hell do you think you're doing, smoking skunk in this house? What are you doing smoking it, full stop?' she yelled, her temper rising.

'Take a chill pill, Ma. If anyone catches me, they'll let me off with a caution. It's not a problem if it's just for personal use,' he drawled with a lop-sided smile.

'Someone has caught you – me, and I won't stand for it. You know the rules, and you've flagrantly broken them. Now, pack a bag and get out. I don't care where you stay but you're not sitting in my house smoking drugs. The next thing I know you'll be injecting them.'

'Cool it. I'd never be that stupid, but what's wrong with a bit of weed?'

'There are new brain cancers being discovered all the time in those old hippies from the sixties who used it. There is evidence that it causes brain damage and changes personalities. It can also cause mental illness and paranoia. And it's *much* stronger than it used to be. Shall I go on?'

'Like you are now?'

'Get out of here and don't come back ...'

'You evil old bitch!' Ben had stood up, and yelled into her face. 'You treat me as if I was three years old. I'm old enough to drink, vote, and get married without your permission. If I want to smoke a little dope, there's nothing you can do to stop me.'

'Someone about your age fell from a roof today and smashed himself to bits on the pavement below because he was high on skunk, or whatever. Do you want to end up like that? Act your age and not your shoe size.'

'You shut your mouth. You're like some sort of Third-

World dictator. Where do you get off telling me what I can and can't do? Just who the hell do you think you are? You're just a plod, and you don't even have the brains to think for yourself.'

'How dare you talk to me like that, you little shit. I'm your mother, God help me …'

'Hey, what's happenin'?' Hal's deep bass growl sounded up the stairs, and soon his head appeared over the bannister. 'Nobody's leaving this house until I find out what's going on.'

There were a lot of angry, hurtful things said that could never be erased, while Hal mediated between mother and son, but they finally reached a truce. Ben promised never to bring the stuff into the house again, to never even dabble in it again, and Olivia promised to try to treat him more like an adult than a rebellious child. Olivia knew she had always felt the need to supervise Ben more closely than Hibbie following some very minor delinquent episodes in his younger teenage years. She had seen enough young lads go off the rails in the course of her career to know how easily they were influenced by peer pressure from who she perceived as budding criminals, and drug use was usually the first step.

In Home Farm Barn that evening, Lauren was dismayed to receive a phone call from her husband telling her that he was in receipt of some unexpected leave, and would be home the next day. As Lauren ended the call, her eyes filled with tears – but not tears of joy. If she was lonely when Kenneth was away, she felt equally as lonely when he came back, if not more so. All he really wanted her for was to be a bit of arm candy if he wanted to go out, and to play the outside of a sausage roll every night. Every night! What other woman would stand for that? Well, she had, and for years now. She wasn't going to stand for it anymore.

He had said he'd ring again from the airport when his flight was called, and if she happened to be out when he arrived home, then it was a case of hard luck. He'd have to make do with pot luck and Gerda. She worked, too, and he didn't show her any respect for what she did.

Back at the cottage, Olivia was sitting at her laptop with the copy of the photofit beside her, looking through pictures of local villains, to see if she recognised anyone having any resemblance to that poor young lad.

Hal came over and looked over her shoulder. 'Still working?' he asked.

'Just looking for a face,' she explained.

Her husband picked up the sheet of paper, and she could hear him draw in his breath with surprise. 'What's up?' she asked.

'I know this kid,' he replied. 'Is this the one you found in that field off the ring road?'

'It is. Who is he?'

'Remember I told you the other night that our regular barman was missing, and there was someone else running the drinks and, if I'm not wrong, running something else as well?'

'Was it him?'

'No, this guy in the picture was the regular one. I thought he'd probably just phoned in sick.'

'What was his name?' Olivia was desperate for this information.

'Everyone knew him as Ricky. If you want a full name and address, you should contact the owner and get him to check staff records.

'Ricky what?'

'I don't know. You'll have to get in touch with the boss.'

'Name?'

'Julian Church. I've got his mobile number somewhere

if you'll give me a minute. I need to phone him if I'm not turning up to a gig for any reason.'

Julian Church answered his mobile after two rings and confirmed that he had a barman by the name of Ricky Dunbar. He also disclosed that Ricky lived with his parents in one of the houses on the big new estate, and that he knew the parents were away at the moment on holiday for some winter sun. 'Ricky hasn't graced us with his presence for a couple of days. Probably holed up at his parents' house with some bird or other, having the time of his life.'

Olivia couldn't recall any female bodies in the mortuary, and kept quiet, asking instead, 'Do you have the actual address?'

'Hang on a moment while I check. Why? What's our Ricky been up to? Nothing naughty, I hope.'

'Just routine enquiries, sir,' lied Olivia, not wanting to spread any more information about than she needed to. 'Do you know when his parents will be back from holiday, by any chance?'

'Tomorrow, I believe, but why don't you just ask Ricky?'

'The address, please, sir, if you have it.'

He had it.

INTERLUDE

The last thing the man remembered had been drinking a pint of lager with one of his dodgy contacts, with whom he had been trying to worm his way into what he considered to be easy money for very little expenditure of effort. He had thought the man was coming round to his persuasions when he had bought the last round of drinks.

Putting down a pint of lager and one of Guinness, the latter before his contact, he went to the gents to relieve his protesting bladder. Nerves had made the first pint go straight through him, then he thought he'd move in for the kill when he returned to the table. He'd already found out enough, here and there, to make it sound as if he knew all about what was going on, and he thought this would be his gateway into a cushy little number.

Not long after he sat down at the table, he drained his glass in an act of masculine bravado, to demonstrate that here was a man not to be messed with, and the other man started to stare at him as if he were an exhibit in a museum. The man smacked his lips, and began to list all that he knew, in the hope that he would be invited to be part of the action, but as he spoke, his tongue felt heavy in his mouth, and he began to slur his words.

He tried to get up to go outside for some air, but his limbs would not co-operate. The other man was watching him more closely than ever, and he managed to slur out, 'Wha're you starin' a'?' as his brain turned to cotton wool. He was aware of his companion signalling to the barman and calling over.

'I wonder if you can give me a hand with my mate. He

seems to have had one over the eight, and I need to get him back to my car so I can return him home to the bosom of his family.'

Except there was no family as such. And he'd only had two pints. Had he been taken suddenly ill?

He was aware of his arms being hoisted over the shoulders of the barman and his contact, and being dragged from the pub, his feet scuffing along the ground behind him. He was vaguely aware that he was being manhandled into the back of a car, but after that, he blacked out.

When consciousness returned, his first reaction was confusion. What had happened after he had left the pub? Where was he? He seemed to be lying on a concrete floor. And why couldn't he move? His arms and legs seemed to be bound, his arms behind his back, his legs at the ankles. He was covered in what he thought might be a dirty tarpaulin stinking of fish. How had he got here? Where was the man he had been having a drink with? What was going to happen to him, and why?

The sound of muffled voices reached him from around first floor height and, turning his head painfully, he saw a glassed-in area that must have once served as an office. He felt like death, as if he were suffering from the worst hangover ever: his head hurt, his mouth was dry, his stomach was churning, but whether this was from fear, or a reaction to whatever had caused this sorry state of affairs, he had no idea. And some of his muscles ached from where he had been dragged around.

The voices got louder, as four figures wearing ski masks left the office at mezzanine height and descended the stairs, three of them making straight for his prone figure, the other collecting something heavy from the underside of the wooden stairway.

'So, this is the nosy little bastard, is it?' growled one, casually aiming a terrific kick at his ribs.

'Aye, that's the miserable little worm trying to muscle in on our act,' replied another, this time aiming a kick that caught him on the forehead.

'Well, fuck you, mister. I think you've just met your nemesis,' hissed the third, this time aiming for the left shoulder with his steel-capped boot. The fourth man joined them and their victim raised his head as far as he could to identify that this figure was dragging a huge sack which seemed to contain something very heavy.

He closed his eyes in disbelief, praying for the first time since he had been a young child. 'Please, God, don't let this be happening. Let me live. I'll do anything if you just get me out of this. Anything.'

'Kick for luck, lads?' said the first man, and the man who had dragged over the sack landed one just above his right kidney, sending a surprising ecstasy of pain shooting through his body. 'Into the sack he goes,' said the first figure again, evidently the highest-ranking in this small group of thugs. The bound man felt his body being lifted up until he was horizontal, then he was slipped into the mouth of the open sack. When his feet hit the bottom he became aware that it was full of what felt like large, heavy stones. What the fuck were they doing to him?

'Round his neck, lads, as tight as you can so he can't get it off. I want him in that bag and helpless.' The sack had obviously been prepared for whatever purpose they had in mind for him, and the two ends of a rope that protruded from holes in the hemming were tied a little too tightly for comfort just above his Adam's apple.

'Check the rope's secure so that he doesn't float away. We want him found and the lesson to be learnt.' The bagged man suddenly became aware that a rope was tied through the one that surrounded his neck. This was getting worse by the minute. Were they going to dangle him from somewhere really high?

'Get him out now and dispose of him. I won't stand for

upstarts like that thinking they can move in on our territory.' His helpless body was lifted and taken through the door to the outside world, where he became aware that they were on the bank of the local river.

'Oh, no, not that!' he screamed in his terror. They were going to throw him into the water. The last breath he took was as he sailed through the air and landed, breaking the surface of the river into myriad ripples and splashes. The stones immediately took him down to the river bed, where the current played carelessly with his body, as he struggled in what he knew would be his last effort in this life. His last conscious thought before he drowned was, 'So where's the whole of my life that's supposed to pass before my mind's eye?'

The man who had fetched the sack secured the end of the rope to a metal mooring ring, and the four of them strolled nonchalantly away, job done.

CHAPTER FOUR

Lauren woke the next morning with a thumping head and a dry mouth. After Kenneth's surprise news, she had taken a bottle of wine to bed, and swallowed the second of the two sleeping tablets that Hal had given her the other night. She had cried herself to sleep after finishing the whole bottle of wine, and was now paying the price for it.

She staggered into the shower, trying to wash off the guilt and disgust she felt at returning to her role as wife, one she had not cherished for a number of years now. She had only enjoyed the children, and now that Jade had gone off to prep school this last September, she felt like she didn't exist anymore, at least not in any real sense, in the home.

After a brisk rub dry, she sat in front of her dressing table mirror carefully applying such make-up as would minimise her red and swollen eyes, then opened her work wardrobe to select a suitably sombre suit for dealing with two young and unnecessary deaths, although at the moment, she felt she ought to add her marriage to the list of the fallen.

Lauren took her time driving to the station. She was not looking forward to leaving the office that night, as Kenneth would be home. She would spend as much time as she could at the end of the working day catching up with any necessary, and maybe even some *un*necessary, paperwork.

DI Hardy was already behind her desk going through what had occurred overnight when she entered. She must put on a brave face, and she did her best to greet her boss with a smile. 'Everything OK?' asked Hardy, instinctively aware that all was not well in Lauren's world.

'Just a bit of a run-in with the au pair, that's all,' she lied, and got away with it.

'If she's not suitable, just give her the old heave-ho. There are plenty of young women, and older ones come to that, who would love the security of a live-in job with not too arduous a schedule.'

'I'll give it some thought,' replied Lauren, aware of a little shake in her voice, and immediately sitting down and starting to go through the paperwork that was in her in tray.

'We've got a name for the kid in the field,' said Hardy, 'Hal recognised his photofit. It's a chap called Ricky Dunbar who worked at the club where Hal plays. We'll go see his parents later.'

At 10.30, Hardy chivvied her sergeant to her feet, saying, 'Come on. I checked with the neighbours to see when Mr and Mrs Dunbar will arrive home from their holiday, and they were due to get to the house just after nine. I doubt they'll be considering going into work today after their overnight journey, so let's get this over with.'

Reluctantly, Lauren rose to her feet, her stomach doing somersaults, her throat dry. She really hated this part of the job, made even worse today given her own unhappy domestic circumstances. Her eyes on her feet, she slipped back into her jacket and followed the DI down to the car park.

At the neat modern Georgian-style terraced house that proved to be the family home of the Dunbars, Mrs Dunbar answered their ring with a neutral face, and gave them the smallest of smiles when she saw that two women stood on the doorstep. 'How can I help you?' she asked, wondering if they were lost and in need of some directions.

'Mrs Dunbar?' Hardy checked, holding out her warrant card. Groves followed suit, and the smile fell away from the woman's face as if it had slid off an icy surface.

'What's happened?' she asked anxiously. 'Is it our Ricky? His bed's not been slept in, and he's such an untidy boy, usually.'

'May we come in please, Mrs Dunbar?' Bad news of the magnitude they were bringing couldn't be blurted out on a doorstep like a cheap piece of gossip.

'What is it? Tell me,' she begged them, standing aside so that they could enter. In silence the two detectives entered the living room, and Hardy nodded at Groves to go into the kitchen to make a cup of tea. She had the feeling that they would all need one by the time they had finished.

'Where's Mr Dunbar?' the inspector enquired.

'He's upstairs finishing the unpacking,' the woman said in a voice that was devoid of all emotion, as if it were she who were dead.

'Can you call him in here, please? I have something to tell you that you both should hear.'

'Oh, my God! Chris! You need to come down here now,' Mrs Dunbar called through the door, a note of panic now infecting her voice.

There was the thump of somebody descending the stairs, a slight break as the man put his head into the kitchen, enquiring who the hell Groves was, and what she was doing in his kitchen. After the higher notes of Groves' voice, he finally entered the living room, his face ashen with dread as he realised that there was a policewoman in the kitchen and, no doubt, this was another one in his living room. It could only bode ill.

'Have you come about Ricky?' he asked, without waiting for the other woman to introduce herself.

'DI Hardy, Mr Dunbar, Mrs Dunbar, and that's DS Groves in the kitchen, making us all a nice cup of tea.'

'Is this about Ricky? Is he in some sort of trouble?' the man persisted, while his wife put a hand up to her mouth in dread anticipation.

At that point she joined the conversation. 'We noticed that his bed didn't seem to have been slept in and a lot of the food I left for him in the freezer is still there. He should have used more of it.'

'I'm afraid it is about Ricky, Mr and Mrs Dunbar. I suggest that you sit down, sir.'

'He's dead, isn't he?' Mrs Dunbar blurted out, and put her hands over her eyes as they filled with anticipatory tears.

'I'm afraid we have reason to believe that the body we have found is that of your son,' replied Hardy as the sobs started to seep out through the bereaved mother's fingers.

'How did it happen?' asked the man. 'Was it an accident on the road? Was he knocked down and killed?' His face was as grey as putty as he asked these almost impossible questions. It seemed unbelievable that they could have returned from a lovely, relaxing holiday to a nightmare like this.

'I'm afraid it's rather more serious than that. I'm sorry to have to inform you but he was murdered.'

'Murdered?'

'How?'

'I think, if it's all right with you, we should leave that till a little later. In the meantime, would you be able to come down to the mortuary and formally identify his body?'

'But how did he die? I have to know. He is ... was ... my son ... our son. We need to know.' Mrs Dunbar was now wailing and keening, and rocking herself backwards and forwards in her seat as grief and shock set in.

'You can't keep the details from us. He was our flesh and blood,' chimed in Mr Dunbar, whose own eyes had filled, and looked as if the pupils would drown in unshed tears.

'I think we'll leave the details until after we've had a

nice cup of tea,' responded Hardy, as Groves entered with a tray in her hands, the cups rocking in their saucers as the sergeant's own nervousness made itself visible. She was always like this when it was a case of breaking bad news: she simply couldn't either avoid it, or get used to it.

Lauren put down the tray on a convenient coffee table, and checked whether they wanted milk and sugar before handing over the cups. When all had been served, she made a banal comment about not knowing where to find the biscuits, then a veil of silence settled over the scene. What could they talk about? It hardly seemed appropriate to ask whether they'd had a good holiday. Coming back from this one would be something they'd never forget.

'Why did we have to go away?' sobbed Mrs Dunbar. 'We never even had the chance to say goodbye. Maybe if we hadn't gone when we did, this would never have happened.'

'There, there, love. We can't live on might-have-beens,' her husband consoled her, rubbing her back in an attempt to comfort her.

'He was only a boy, really. We should have taken him with us.'

'He wouldn't have come, love. We both know that. He may have been a boy to you, but he was an adult in the eyes of the law.'

'I don't give a shit about the eyes of the law! My baby boy is dead, and you try to comfort me like that.' Her voice had risen in pitch and volume, and her husband suddenly knelt down beside her chair, and gathered her to his chest, holding her tightly as she wailed and struggled.

'Can you tell me where I can find your doctor's number, Mr Dunbar? I think your wife should be looked at, and possibly given something to calm her down' said Hardy quietly.

'In the address book by the phone in the hall,' he replied, 'under U for Underhill.'

Hardy nodded slightly in Groves' direction, and she put down her cup, got up and left the room, closing the door into the hall behind her. 'Mrs Dunbar could certainly do with a little chemical help to get her through the next few days. I think it would be better if you went on your own to identify your son's body, Mr Dunbar. Is there someone we could contact to sit with your wife after the doctor's been?'

'Her sister lives just the other side of the town centre. Her number's in the same address book under F for Filey, Mrs Judith Filey.'

'I'll tell my sergeant as soon as she's finished calling the doctor, and she can arrange for her to come over.'

'If she doesn't answer the landline, her mobile number's in there as well,' said Mr Dunbar, tears now coursing down his cheeks as he rocked with his wife as they expressed their grief and sorrow.

Within ten minutes, Dr Underhill arrived and was left ministering to his patient as the other three people in the house retired discreetly to the dining room. When he had finished, he called them back through and handed a small bottle to Mr Dunbar. 'I've given her a sedative for now. This bottle has some sleeping tablets in it to help her get through the night, and I suggest that you take one, too. This has been an appalling shock for you both. I'd like to call back in the morning to see how you both are.'

He shook hands with the bereaved man and, as he was leaving, a car pulled on to the drive containing Judith Filey. A woman evidently in some distress got out of the car, and rushed towards the still open door, where she engulfed her brother-in-law in a hug.

'God, how awful this is. Where's Mary? How is she?'

'Not good,' replied Clive Dunbar, hugging his sister-in-law back. 'You'd better go through to her. I have to go with these policewomen to identify Ricky's body.'

'What happened to him?' the newcomer asked.

'I don't know the details as yet, but the officers said they'd tell me on the way to the mortuary.'

At the sound of that dread word, Judith Filey suddenly let loose her tears as she realised that this was all real and not just some stupid prank.

Interrupting at this point, Hardy announced that she was going to radio in for a constable to come and sit with the two women until Mr Dunbar returned and break the news of how their son had died to his wife, and they would play it by ear until then.

As the car left for the mortuary, which was at the hospital, nearly ten miles away, Groves drove, and DI Hardy sat in the back with Mr Dunbar, slowly explaining about what he could expect to find when they got there.

'I'm afraid your son's not a pretty sight, Mr Dunbar. It would appear that he was beaten very badly ante-mortem, then left in a field to die. I don't know how much of this you will decide to discuss with your wife, but you must be prepared for there to be some pretty gory details appearing in the local press. It would be better coming from you, than her finding out from a local news report or from the local paper. When the constable arrives, she will do her best to be gentle about what she tells your wife.'

'Oh, God, I hadn't even thought about that ... can you stop the car, please,' he asked very politely, adding, 'Quickly,' with more urgency.

Groves pulled over on to a grass verge, and Mr Dunbar opened the door and was flamboyantly and ingloriously sick. When he had reached the stage of dry heaving, Hardy rubbed one of his shoulders in comfort, then waited for him to sit back up and close the door.

'I'm so sorry about that.'

'It's only to be expected, sir, after such dreadful news. Drive on, Groves.'

At the hospital they approached the mortuary entrance, Dunbar's footsteps at first quick, as if to get this dreadful thing over with as soon as possible. Then, as they reached the entrance, he slowed to a snail's pace in dread and fear at what he would have to confront.

'Come along, Mr Dunbar. You'll only be shown his face for the purposes of identification. Let's get it over with so that you can go back to your wife. She's in great need of you at this tragic time.' The words may have sounded trite to Hardy's ears, but they represented good common sense and, taking a huge breath to brace himself, he increased his walking pace to normal.

They led him to a glass-walled room, on the other side of which lay a hospital trolley covered in a white sheet. Dunbar thought that he had never seen such a fearful sight in his life, or one more intimidating and threatening as that covered form underneath all that pristine whiteness, and he began to shake, dreading what was about to happen.

'Don't be afraid, Mr Dunbar. You'll feel better for doing this. At least it won't let your imagination conjure up anything worse, and at least you'll know.'

'What do I do if my wife says she wants to see him?' he asked, a quiver of uncertainty in his voice.

'If you think she's up to it after you've made the identification, then of course she can come and view her son's body. It might be a good idea if you left it a day or two, though.'

It was Dr MacArthur the FME himself who entered the room and pulled back the sheet to uncover the face. Mr Dunbar took a good look, then yelped like a kicked puppy. He paled to the colour of milk. 'Yes, that's our Ricky, God bless his soul.'

'Catch him, Groves,' barked Hardy, as the man crumpled towards the floor. DS Groves caught him under the armpits as he went down – thank God she was a tall officer – and Dr MacArthur rushed out of the room to find a chair to rest him on.

'Well fielded, Groves. We'll make a cricketer out of

you yet,' Hardy congratulated her. It wouldn't do to bring this poor man home with a concussion. He'd been through enough as it was.

Dr MacArthur opened his mouth to make some comments on the injuries to the young man's body, but was effectively silenced by Hardy who delivered a swift kick to his right shin. 'This man's been through hell today, Dylan. Don't make it any the worse for him by saying things that are bound to give him nightmares. I'll speak to you on the phone later, and you can spout forth to your heart's content to me.'

Draping an arm each of Dunbar's round their shoulders, and making quite an off-kilter sight with their difference in height, they assisted him back to the car, leaving the FME rubbing his shin and swearing under his breath about police brutality.

Dunbar was recovered a little by the time they returned to his home, and they found the female officer and Judith Filey sitting on the sofa in the living room with Mrs Dunbar, comforting her. As they entered, Mrs Dunbar shot to her feet.

'I want to see him, too,' she announced immediately. 'It was him, wasn't it, Clive, and not some dreadful mistake?'

'It's him, Mary love, but I've seen him and he's at peace now.'

'Then I can go, too?' Her face was unnaturally eager in the circumstances, and, thought Hardy, her body language made imminent hysteria a distinct possibility.

'Not today, love. Maybe tomorrow,' replied her husband wearily. It was only early afternoon, but he felt as if the day had already lasted forever.

'You promise? Promise me, Clive!' shrieked Mrs Dunbar, confirming what Hardy had thought of her current mental state. Judith Filey interrupted at this point to say, 'I've persuaded Mary that she and Clive ought to come to

stay with me, just for a few days while things settle down.'
She had foreseen an intense press interest, and thought that
it would be better if they weren't available to anyone from
the media that cared to call at their home.

'I've got a different surname, so there's no way the
press could find me easily. And I think they could do with
the company. I'll phone their workplaces and sort
everything out, and I'll take a few days off myself. They'll
be in good hands, Inspector.'

Hardy heartily agreed with this suggestion. As they
were preparing to leave for Judith's, the uniformed
constable offered to go with them, but the two women said
it wasn't necessary, although Hardy recommended it for a
couple of hours at least, so that they could ask any further
questions that occurred to them.

Once Hardy and Groves arrived back at the office, there
was the usual stuff to deal with, things that Uniform could
handle for now: shoplifting, aggressive begging, domestic
fallouts. The events of the morning had done nothing to lift
Groves's spirits at the imminent arrival of her husband,
soon to be back to the bosom – and a few other parts – of
his wife, and she would do everything within her power to
prolong her working day.

Having ascertained that the uniformed officers were
dealing with the domestics, Groves took a break for
lunch – a very late lunch as it happened – promising to
interview those shoplifters arrested during the course of
the morning when she came back. She took her full hour,
eating in a small café that specialised in liver and bacon,
enjoying one of their generous servings with the wry
thought that the condemned woman ate a hearty lunch,
before returning to the station to string out the interviews
she would conduct that afternoon, spinning them out for as
long as possible.

When every guest in their 'special rooms' had been

dealt with, she went back to her desk to type up the notes, something that should have been delegated to a more junior officer, but which she attacked slowly and with the thought that her late arrival home would probably keep Kenneth off her back – or at least her front – until it was time for bed.

When DI Hardy packed up and shut down her computer, she called over to Lauren that she wouldn't get any overtime for all this extra work as the budget was stretched tighter than an old film star's face, but the sergeant just waved and carried on with her work. When she was finally alone in the office, she finished off her notes then made herself a good, hot, strong cup of coffee and pulled her e-reader out of her handbag.

It was only common sense to come to work prepared. Sometimes things took a lot of waiting for, and this was her secret weapon against boredom. Now, she used it to ward off the evil hour for as long as possible, when she would have to return home. Finally, she looked at her watch and decided she really ought to leave. It was eight o'clock, and by the time they'd eaten or, if the au pair from hell had already fed Kenneth, eaten something herself, it would be almost time to surrender to the inevitable.

Pushing her horn-rimmed glasses back up her nose, she grabbed her handbag and jacket, and walked very slowly down to the car park, her stomach churning with dread at the ordeal that she knew awaited her. Taking the long route home, she drove as slowly as she could, and finally opened the front door at half past eight, her hands actually shaking as she tried to get her key back out of the lock.

Kenneth came bounding out of the open-plan living space with a smile on his face, and wearing only a bathrobe and the mules he had adopted as slippers. He engulfed her in a bear hug, then kissed her with enthusiasm and rather a lot of tongue which, she found, turned her stomach. How long could she carry on with this charade?

'Kenneth, I'm tired and hungry. Let me come in and get something to eat before you start pawing at me,' she said in her bravest voice.

'But I haven't seen you in months,' he protested.

'Not now, Kenneth. I presume, from your friskiness, that you've had a nap since you got back.'

A sly smile pulled at the corners of his mouth as he agreed that he had indeed been to bed since he'd returned. At that point Gerda sidled out of the living room, similarly attired to Kenneth and with the satisfied expression of a cat that's got the cream, the milk, and the chicken breasts.

'Have you been in the bath?' asked Lauren suspiciously.

'I thought I'd have an early night but I came downstairs to keep Kenneth company until you got back from your precious job,' she replied insolently.

'We've already eaten,' added Kenneth, suppressed triumph in his voice, and Lauren's face turned stony as she stalked off into the kitchen to microwave herself something acceptably hot but, inevitably, bland.

She left the two of them in the living room watching what sounded like an American film with lots of car chases, shouting, and shooting. Kenneth called through to her asking if she'd like a glass of wine, but she declined; she simply wasn't in the mood. After she had eaten, she took the back stairs up to the bedroom, taking her e-reader with her.

If she snuck off like this, it would delay Kenneth's hour of retiring, and leave her in peace for just a little precious time longer, unmolested, and lost in the book she was currently reading. She could hear Kenneth's heavy footsteps on the main stairs at ten o'clock, but continued to read, hoping he'd be too tired after his overnight flight, and had started to suffer from jetlag.

Her luck was out, however, and he looked as perky as

ever when he entered the room. As he shed his bathrobe, revealing that he was wearing nothing underneath it, he got into bed, and she could smell the alcohol on his breath. He'd either drunk the whole bottle himself, or he'd shared it with Gerda. Yes, she decided, they probably had shared it, as there was still a twinkle in his eye that boded nothing good for her.

A few minutes later she lay on her back, as Kenneth pumped away at her body, grunting and groaning like an animal, totally absorbed in his own pleasures, while tears ran down the sides of her face as she endured this rutting ritual – because that was all it was – for the first time in months.

When he'd finished, he rolled off her, turning his back, and almost immediately started to snore. Lauren slipped from under the sheets, put on her dressing-gown and made for Gerda's room to see if there was any truth in what she suspected about that little foreign bitch and Kenneth. She thought that Gerda had looked much too smug when she arrived home from work, and Kenneth would normally have wanted to have his selfish way with his wife at least twice on the day of his return. Maybe he'd already had a feed of his oats elsewhere before she got home.

As she approached the young woman's room she heard a soft singing, and took this as the second bit of evidence she had uncovered; the first being the little smile that had hovered at the edges of Kenneth's lips when they stood in the hall together. Without the courtesy of knocking, given the circumstances of her state of mind, she burst through the door like an avenging angel and asked her outright if she had been sleeping with her husband.

Gerda answered, at first, only with a smile, but her tongue was soon loosened when Lauren grabbed her by the lapels of her towelling robe and pulled her up from her seat on the dressing-table stool. 'Tell me, you sly little bitch, are you sleeping with my husband?' As she asked this she shook the younger woman backwards and forwards, her own face a murderous mask. Maybe she didn't love Kenneth anymore, but he was still her husband, and it made her sick to think of the two of them in bed together under this roof.

'How long has this been carrying on? Come on, tell me, you little slapper. Tell me, or so help me, I'll swing for you.' Letting go of her terry-towelling hand-holds, Lauren slapped the au pair soundly round the face, then stood back and waited for her to say something, suddenly aware that she was breathing as if she'd been running. She hadn't realised how territorial she was.

To her total surprise, Gerda struck back at her, catching her on the right cheek. 'You naïve little cow,' spat Gerda. 'This has been going on since the week after I arrived! We're very discreet and have never let the children catch us in bed, but don't be fooled, we've been at it like rabbits.'

Lauren stared at her in disbelief, then took a deep breath and launched herself at this picture of victory, grabbing her by the hair and dragging her down to the ground, where she began to kick at her with her bare feet. Gerda grabbed her by the ankle and brought her down too, managing to disentangle the painful handfuls of hair that her opponent held, and getting back to her feet, she fled from the room to where she knew Kenneth was.

Lauren had hit her face and split her lip in the fall, and was feeling decidedly woozy as she regained an upright position. This, then, was the end of her marriage, was it? She let her thoughts wander back to her previous time in bed with Kenneth that evening and shuddered. This wasn't a minute too soon in coming, when she reflected on how she really felt about him. Gerda was welcome to him, but he wasn't getting custody of her children, and he wasn't getting off lightly financially, either. She'd take him for every penny he'd got, by God.

Mustering every ounce of courage she possessed, she shook her head to clear it, and also made off for the master suite, where she would pack a bag and leave for the rest of the night. It wasn't too late, and she was sure that Olivia would put her up, even if it was just on the sofa.

When she arrived at, what until now, had been her bedroom, the two of them were in bed together, without an ounce of shame between them. She sucked at her split lip as she put together some clothes and toiletries, not forgetting her trusty e-reader, and growled, with all the venom she could muster, 'You'll pay for this, buddy,' as she left the room.

INTERLUDE

It had taken longer than they had thought to dig such a deep hole in the sand, but there was no one about on such a cold night, and there was cloud cover, limiting the natural light. Finally it was done, and the trussed and gagged bundle, lying just behind a rock to shield any view of it from the promenade, was ready for its fate.

Had they been interrupted during their task they would have passed it off as digging for rare lugworms, but no one had passed since they had begun their task. They were at the end of the prom where the houses ended and gave way to municipal gardens – not somewhere to stroll after the hours of darkness, when the place was locked up anyway.

Taking a quick look round to see that they were not being watched, they dragged the man over the sand and held his head over the hole, shining a torch down it to show him how deep they had dug. Immediately he began to struggle and moan, imagining that he would be lowered in feet first and left to drown when the tide came in.

How wrong he was. To his utter surprise and horror, they dragged him to his feet, and lowered him in head first, the deepness of the hole dampening the groaned protests that escaped through his gagged mouth. Slowly the sand was replaced, filling first that part of the hole where his head was located. The world became darker and darker, until he found he couldn't breathe, and he knew he was done for.

They had not even finished filling the hole when the purposely visible feet gave a final jerk, and then were still.

'Another one bites the dust.'

That was the only comment, and the men tamped down their handiwork and walked off the beach, heading for the various places that they laid their heads for the night.

This one had not been so much fun, because they had had to stay around and listen to the man slowly suffocate. It would have been better if they could have arranged it with a different scenario; one where they could walk away and just leave their victim to die, and not have to be there as it happened.

Even the most evil of characters have their limits of tolerance, and can only stomach so much.

CHAPTER FIVE

Afterwards, Lauren could never recall that drive to Olivia's house. Blinded with tears, she was also suffering from a deep shock that things could have come to a head so suddenly and catastrophically. She had envisaged a civilised talk about how she and Kenneth had drifted apart and how it would be better if he got himself a little flat, or even stayed in the granny annexe when he was in the UK, so that he could maintain his relationship with the children, such as it was.

This sudden acceleration of events, culminating in the shocking discovery that he had been sleeping with the evil au pair almost since she had started her employment with them, had been a completely out-of-the-blue revelation to her, and she felt mentally numb with disbelief. How could this have been going on under her nose? Would things have been different if she had been a stay-at-home mum who needed just the domestic assistance of a cleaner? How much of it was her fault?

When she finally knocked on Olivia's door clutching her holdall, she became aware that she had not brushed her hair, that there were tears streaming down her face, her nose was running unchecked, and her lip was swollen and still bleeding from her tussle with the enemy. Whatever would the guv'nor say at her appearance, unannounced and in a state, at this time of night?

What Olivia said, quite sympathetically, was, 'What the hell happened to you?' – but her face had been stern when she first opened the door, before she realised who was calling on her so late. Although Lauren was only marginally aware of them, Olivia had mounting troubles of her own.

'Come on in, Lauren. No, you're not disturbing us at all. We're never in bed early. You look like you could do with a drink to steady you. Glass of wine be OK?'

'Thank you,' mumbled Lauren, sliding down onto a sofa. She felt drained and exhausted, barely able to put coherent thoughts together.

'White all right?' the DI's voice called from the kitchen, and Lauren grunted in acceptance. Reappearing with a tray with three glasses of wine on it, Olivia put it down on a coffee table and handed one to her sergeant. 'Hal's just getting his kit together for a gig tomorrow night. He's upstairs, but he'll join us shortly.'

Lauren stared at her boss dumbly, not having the energy to say a word. 'Get that glass of wine down you and try to relax a little, and we'll talk whenever you're ready. If you want to stay here tonight, you're welcome to have Hibbie's room. She's still staying with her friend, and I've already stripped the beds and put on clean sheets. She should be back in a couple of days, but you're welcome to stay here until you get whatever it is sorted out.'

Lauren drained the glass of wine in one long gulp, then held it out for a refill. At the moment she didn't care how ill-mannered that looked: all her veneer of good manners, painstakingly applied to her at home with her own nanny and at her private school, had fallen away in that bedroom with Gerda and, at the moment, she felt as savage as some of the losers that made her professional life so unnecessarily difficult.

When she had drained her second glass and it had been refilled for a second time, she felt ready to speak but before she could, Hal's voice sounded from upstairs, with a note of real panic in it. 'Phone an ambulance. Dial 999 *now*.'

'What is it?' shouted the inspector.

'Don't waste a second. Make that phone call right this minute.'

He sounded so panicky that Olivia did as she was told without any more questions, and Lauren sat as still as a statue, thinking that maybe she had chosen the wrong moment to come here to unburden herself.

As Olivia looked around for the phone, Lauren rose and called up the stairs, 'What shall she tell them, Hal?

'Suspected drugs overdose. He's unconscious. Tell Liv.'

But Liv had already heard, and was in the process of ringing for an ambulance. She was taking no chances with her son's life. When she ended the call she shot straight upstairs, taking only a second to glance apologetically towards Lauren. Some things had to take precedence, and this was one of them.

Lauren sat quite still sipping at her third glass of wine, aware of a howl of denial from upstairs, then of the thundering of heavy feet back downstairs. Hal rushed through the room, muttering 'coffee', and made a cup in the kitchen, using instant granules and the hottest water the tap could provide. This was no time for boiling kettles and preparing cafetières; this was an emergency.

Running back up the stairs, trying not to spill his liquid offering, she heard the sound of panicky voices and could imagine the scene upstairs. Olivia would have put her son in the recovery position and would be talking to him, trying desperately to keep him going …

There was nothing practical she could do, so she just sat there nursing her glass and wishing that she smoked – at least she would have something to do with her hands, and the nicotine would help soothe her frayed nerves.

The ambulance arrived exactly seven and a half minutes later, as the ambulance station was only a short distance away in the town, and the place was suddenly swarming with paramedics, a trolley being manoeuvred up

the narrow turned staircase to assist the crew down with –
what was his name? – Ben's body; no, no, she mustn't
refer to him as a body. He wasn't dead, merely unwell.

She was only aware of a sort of scuffling noise from
above, accompanied by low voices, so she assumed they
were working on the boy on the floor of his room. Shortly
afterwards, two paramedics started the descent of the
awkward staircase, Ben strapped to their seat-trolley,
Olivia and Hal following behind, their faces ashen and
grave.

'I'll go in the ambulance with him and deal with all the
booking-in procedure. You follow in a short while, when
they've got him on a ward or whatever,' Hal advised.

'But he's my son,' replied Olivia in a strangled squeak.

'He's my son, too,' retorted Hal, following the last
paramedic out of the house and closing the door behind
him.

Olivia collapsed into an armchair and stared ahead of
her blankly, unaware of anything else other than that her
son's life may be in danger: she may have to prepare
herself to lose him.

After giving her a couple of minutes undisturbed,
Lauren asked quietly, her own problems temporarily
forgotten in the drama of the present situation, 'Have you
any idea what he took?'

'Not at the moment, but Hal said one of his friends had
been round for a couple of hours before I came home and,
although he seems a well-brought-up lad, Hal just thinks
there's something iffy about him. I know who he is and
where he lives, so I'm going to phone his house.' A quick
riffle through the telephone directory gave her the number
she needed.

She grabbed the phone and started to dial. 'Just speak
calmly,' warned Lauren as the number was ringing,
earning herself a look that indicated that the boss was well
aware of how to handle the conversation without outside

74

help.

After a few minutes of fairly hushed conversation during which Olivia kept her cool admirably, she ended the call. 'That bloody junkie woman!' she practically screamed.

'What is it?' asked Lauren cautiously. She didn't want her boss to come down on her like a ton of bricks, just to vent her spleen about someone else.

'She had a look at her hoard of dangerous drugs and questioned her son about some that were missing, and discovered that he'd made off with a load of old-fashioned sleeping tablets that no doctor not in his dotage would prescribe now, *and* a load of Valium. I'll have to phone the hospital before I leave, so that they can be prepared.'

'Let me come with you,' said Lauren quietly. She had rushed over here for comfort concerning her own problems and discovered that Olivia's were just as serious and rather more immediate.

'No. I could be there all night. One of us has to be fresh enough to go into the office tomorrow. By the way, why did you come over? You looked upset.'

'It doesn't matter, for now,' replied Lauren honestly, and it really didn't. There was a way out of her hole, but if things went belly up with her son Olivia could well be facing a hole of a completely different sort – one about six feet deep …

'I'll be off then. If Hibbie comes home tell her she'll have to sleep either in our bed or on the sofa. And don't lock up. We'll need to get in when we get back.'

Having phoned the hospital, the stumpy figure of DI Hardy left the house, and Lauren was left on her own, her only immediate plans to finish her wine, have a quick look round for some more of the medication Hal had given her on her previous visit, and then go up to bed. Hibbie's room should be easy enough to identify.

She took her holdall upstairs, easily finding the girl's

bedroom, and put down the pills she'd located from her hand on to the bedside table, heading first for the shower before she went to bed.

The sound of the door opening woke her just after four, followed by two pairs of footsteps mounting the staircase with evident caution. The Hardys had obviously not forgotten their unexpected overnight guest. Their footsteps mingled with their low voices and Lauren couldn't resist pulling on a baggy jumper, one she had grabbed in her quick pack, and rushing out of the bedroom.

'How is he?' She blurted out the question, only afterwards, thinking what if the news were not good? To her utter relief, Olivia and Hal both smiled tiredly at her, and Hal said, 'It looks like he's going to be all right.'

'We'll tell you all about it after a couple of hours' kip,' said Olivia. 'We're a bit bushed at the moment, but there's no need to panic anymore. The emergency is over, although it was touch and go, for a while.' With that, her two hosts disappeared into their own bedroom, and she could hear them getting undressed.

She slunk back into the room she considered her own, as a temporary measure, and got back under the covers, only now realising how cold her legs and feet had got while she was standing on the landing. She eventually went back to sleep, and it was the alarm on her mobile phone that woke her at half past seven.

After showering, she dressed in the tidiest set of clothes that she had flung into her holdall and, applying a little make-up to cover her still red and puffy eyes, she dragged a brush through her not-quite-dry hair, applied a quick squirt of perfume, and took a look at herself in the mirror on the wardrobe door. She'd do.

Knowing there was instant coffee in the kitchen, Lauren made a hurried breakfast of a cup of this, and a slice of toast, before scribbling a quick note on the notepad by the telephone and placing it on the kitchen table, weighted down by the salt cellar, then slipped out of the house, not quite knowing what to do, but knowing that Olivia would contact her sometime during the day to keep her up to date.

When she arrived at the office everything was as normal, but after a while there was a hum of conversation round the desks of the DCs, until someone spoke up and asked her if she knew where the DI was today. With maximum discretion, she informed them that DI Hardy wouldn't be in the office that morning, but would call later to let them know whether she'd be in that afternoon. Assuring them that she didn't know why the boss was absent, she put her head down and tried to get on with a little investigation about what had happened to Ricky Dunbar.

Her train of thought was interrupted by a message that there had been a report of a body buried in the sand on the beach. The uniformed constable who had taken the report, PC Liam Shuttleworth, thought it was a leg-pull, and that the lads who told him had buried one of their mates up to his neck, then left him, telling him that the tide would get him. It wouldn't be the first time that had happened, and it wouldn't be the last either.

They'd seemed so genuine however that he'd deigned to have a look, and what he'd found chilled him to the bone. Someone had indeed been buried on the beach, but it wasn't *up* to the neck, it was *down* to the feet, which were the only visible parts of whoever it was. Shuttleworth felt his stomach writhe as he took in the sight, and immediately called for back-up and medical assistance, although he was sure the latter would be too late for this victim.

A car with two uniformed officers arrived and spewed out the figures of PC Lenny Franklin, a man nearing retirement age who had always been happy with his lowly rank, and PC Teri Friend, so handy for unexpected callouts. They both approached the lone figure of Shuttleworth as he guarded his gruesome buried treasure, and as they did so the car of Dr MacArthur arrived.

He loped toward the little group that had just formed, his grey curls blown hither and thither as he crossed the open expanse of sand. Whatever was going on he wanted to be in at the kill, as it were. He looked at the feet sticking up, as if in imitation of paper flags pasted onto sticks, and tut-tutted. 'Very nasty. Have you got a CSI team on the way?' said the doctor, squatting to take a closer look at the feet and feel them for temperature, although what that could determine at the arse-end of the year he wasn't quite sure. He was simply intrigued, never having seen a murder quite like this before. He'd read of cases where people had been buried up to their necks and left for the tide to finish them off, but he'd never read about someone buried up to the feet and left to suffocate.

In Hardy's absence, Lauren had driven down to the beach as soon as she heard about the incident, and wasn't sad to leave the details of Ricky Dunbar's gruesome demise behind her. What she found when she got there was absolutely sickening, however, and the sight of those lone feet made her gag. Teri Friend also looked a bit green around the gills, and even the large bulk of Liam Shuttleworth seemed somehow subdued. Only Lenny Franklin, of the police presence, was unmoved. At his age he'd seen everything there was to be seen, and was not easily disturbed. His only comment so far had been, 'Shit sure does seem to happen in these parts.'

When the photographer had taken stills and a short video, showing the position of the body in relationship to the promenade and the municipal gardens, the two PCs who had made a quick trip to the gardens to borrow a couple of shovels began the task of freeing the man from his sandy grave.

When the body finally lay on the sand, as bruised and

battered as Ricky Dunbar had been but at least freed from its beach tomb, Lenny Franklin took one look at the face and said, 'I know that geezer, but I can't remember where from.'

'How can you, Len?' asked Dylan MacArthur, scrutinising the contorted and empurpled features of the dead man.

'You've never seen most of your customers in that there morgue alive, and wouldn't recognise them if you did, but I've seen this fellow before, and him being dead doesn't mean that I can't remember what he used to look like before he went into that hole.'

Lauren had composed herself enough to instruct Franklin to wrack his brains until he came up with a name. After all, this was the second gruesome murder in just a few days, and the same people may be responsible.

Why go to all the trouble that these people had taken, whoever they were, if they weren't making a point? And to whom were they making this point? Were they sending a message? Don't mess with us? Passing psychopaths were characters from lurid fiction, not real life, and she was convinced that these murders had a local origin. There were some very evil people out there, and it was her job to catch them.

A small shiver ran down her spine at the very thought, but she had to pull herself together and get on with this, as she would any other murder investigation. She just hoped that Hardy returned to the office in the near future, so that she could take over as SIO.

At that precise moment, Olivia Hardy was with her husband at her son's bedside. They had suffered a terrible shock the night before when the doctor repeatedly shook Ben to try to get him to breathe. The information about what he might have taken was helpful, but as he lay there in the A&E department with no shoes on, his socks filthy, and his T-shirt not much better, he looked like a homeless orphan. How could they not have seen him getting into this state?

The doctor had told them that if he hadn't been found when he was, he wouldn't have survived for much longer, and it was lucky someone had gone into his room. Olivia had been too panic-stricken to ask Hal why he'd gone in there, as it wasn't something they normally did. Their son was eighteen, and he insisted that his room was his private space which should never be entered by either of his parents. As she waited on the ward, Olivia decided to give it a good turn-out as soon as she could, to make sure there were no more drugs or drug paraphernalia in it. When it was decided that Ben was well enough to be transferred to a side ward for close observation, they finally went home, and slept like the dead until ten o'clock, when they rose, famished. They immediately headed to the kitchen and grabbed a bowl of cereal and a mug of instant coffee each.

Noticing the rinsed cup, plate, and knife on the draining board, Olivia remembered that they'd had an overnight guest. Where was Lauren? The evidence suggested that she'd already got up and gone into work, but she couldn't be sure – not until she noticed the note on the table under the salt cellar.

There was no time to check in with her, though, as she and Hal needed to get back to the hospital as quickly as possible, to see whether Ben's condition had improved or deteriorated. A telephone call in advance had only informed them that the patient was 'comfortable', which meant precisely nothing. It was just hospital chewing gum to stop things kicking off at the other end of the phone.

When her own mother had been paralysed by a stroke and was a victim to advanced Alzheimer's disease, Olivia recalled, the nursing staff had always told her aunt, who phoned once a week, that she was fine. Being 'fine' or 'comfortable' wasn't the same as being in a condition of recovery, nor even the likelihood of it.

When they arrived they were told that the doctor would speak to them shortly. Ben was in a room of his own, next to the nurses' station, and it had a glass wall through which he could be constantly watched to make sure that he didn't relapse into unconsciousness.

When they were given permission to enter the room, their son was in a clean hospital gown and under the top covers, and not in the tramp-like state of dress in which he had arrived. A wave of shame at his earlier appearance washed over Olivia, and she felt tears pricking the back of her eyes – but she could change nothing, and would have to put on a brave face for her son; her baby, once upon a time.

Ben appeared to be asleep, so they sat, one each side of his bed, and watched him for a few minutes, as he breathed easily and regularly. Tears of relief poured unchecked down Hal's face as he sent up a private prayer of thanksgiving. His mother had raised him as a member of the evangelical church, and, whatever his wife's scathing comments about it, his faith was still strong.

Olivia got up and bent over to kiss her son's cheek, then softly stroked his forehead. His eyelids fluttered, and then drew back as he opened his eyes and stared blankly at the ceiling. He said nothing, and Olivia immediately began to worry about brain damage, which had not so far been mentioned.

'Ben?' she bent to whisper in his ear, 'It's Mum and Dad come to visit you. How are you feeling?'

'I'm here too, son,' said Hal in a pleading voice, worried beyond all reason at the blank and unresponsive expression on his son's face, and the lack of recognition in his eyes.

A voice from the doorway broke into their anxious thoughts. 'Don't be worried. We lightly sedated him because he got a bit confrontational when he came round, and we thought it would do him good to sleep it off some more. He'll be fine by this afternoon, if you want to visit him again then. He'll probably be a bit more rational by then, with a little extra time for his brain to recover.'

Turning round they saw what they presumed was a doctor in the doorway to the room. He looked so young they half-expected him to have a plastic stethoscope and a Ladybird book of symptoms sticking out of his pocket. 'I'm the SHO on your son's case. He had a very close shave, and we've lined up a psychiatrist to have a word with him when he's fully conscious again, to make sure that he didn't intend to take his own life.'

'What?' Olivia was shocked almost into speechlessness.

'He'd never do that! He doesn't have any responsibilities or cares. He still lives at home,' countered Hal.

'You'd be surprised at what kids worry about, and his life probably isn't the open book that you think it is. Young people can get into all kinds of messes, then be too scared or frightened to talk to their parents about it. Is he a regular drug user?'

'Of course he's not,' stated Olivia, now shocked into indignation.

'And just how do you know that?' the SHO continued. It was beginning to feel more like an interrogation. 'Does he spend every evening and night at home? Is he around all the time at the weekends? Kids can get up to all sorts of dangerous stuff that their parents couldn't even imagine.'

After a short interval of silence, Olivia was honest enough to admit that since he had started at college, Ben was often away all night and hardly ever spent an evening or weekend at home – and, even when he did, he shut himself into his bedroom, which he had forbidden them to enter.

'Have you ever caught him either in possession of or

taking drugs?'

'I caught him once quite recently smoking a spliff in his bedroom and I was absolutely furious, mainly because of how it could affect my position professionally, and I just didn't think he'd be that stupid after all I've told him about the addicts I've had to deal with.'

'Maybe that's why he's hidden the majority of what he does from you, he's conscious of your job. He probably feels very hemmed in, and taking drugs might be more a way of rebelling than anything else.'

'When we get home we're going through his room to see what else he's got hidden away in there. I can't go through this again. We shouldn't need to watch him as if he were a toddler again.'

'We can always arrange psychological help for him if it seems appropriate,' said the SHO. 'Anyway, I think we should leave the discussion of what has happened, and how to deal with it, until this afternoon, so that your son can join in.'

As one, the parents stood up to leave the room, their son gently snoring in the bed, and left the hospital in silence. Once in the car park, Olivia and Hal turned to one another.

'Psychiatrist?'

'Suicide?'

They avoided starting a conversation until they had driven home. This needed some time to sink in. Had they really neglected him so much that he had got into drugs just to be noticed? All sorts of sources of guilty possibility swirled round Olivia's head as they headed back to Littleton-on-Sea, which was about ten miles away.

Back in their cottage, Hal made coffee on automatic pilot. Olivia, despite her anxiety about her son, felt it necessary to check in with Lauren to let her know what was happening and to find out what was going on in the murder investigation. She was dismayed to learn of the new murder.

'I've got it covered, boss,' said Lauren, although she felt less than comfortable being the SIO, 'you do what you need to do before coming back.'

'I feel so guilty leaving you alone,' said Olivia, 'but thanks for the breathing space. Do you have all the necessary support you need for now?'

'Yes, and Lenny Franklin thinks he may know the victim, so that will be followed up later. See you when you're ready.'

Olivia put the phone down, thinking yet again how difficult it could be to balance work with family. It seemed like she was always walking a fine line between the two.

She cut some sandwiches in absolute silence. Only when the plates were in the sink and the cups refilled did she and Hal begin to talk about how they could have found themselves in the middle of such an unbelievable situation.

When they had got to the bottom of it, there would probably have to be alterations to both their schedules, with a bit more active parenting involved. Then again, the boy was eighteen. If he'd gone away to college and lived in halls, would this still have happened, or was it a symptom of feeling trapped, living with his parents?

When the scenario on the sands had been wrapped up and the body taken away to the rapidly filling mortuary, Lenny Franklin headed back to the station as quick as he could, eager to speak to Monty Fairbanks, the archivist. He was the fount of all local knowledge, even more so than Lenny himself, and he felt that if he described the victim to Monty, he'd be presented with a name straight away.

If *he* had recognised him, Monty would be sure to, and the small tattoo of a spider's web on the victim's neck was a useful identifying feature. He just hoped Monty was on duty.

He was, and after a brief description of build,

approximate height, hair colour, and the additional information of the tattoo, Monty immediately came up with a name. 'Doug Green! Yeo Close, up on the council estate. Been a bit of a jack-the-lad for years, but never got himself into really hot water. I've got him in my card index system.

'Yes, I know it's all supposed to go on computer, but I do like to keep the old cards up to date. So helpful, if you can't be bothered to turn on the blasted machine, and then wait for the valve to warm up; then there's the password to remember. No, I rely on my old cards when I want a name quickly, but I can pull his computer record up for you, Lenny. He's never been convicted of anything, but he's managed to wriggle out of quite a few charges over the years.'

The promise was no sooner made than accomplished, and it wasn't long before Lenny found himself looking at a mugshot of the man discovered murdered on the beach earlier that day.

'I'll pass his details on to one of the female officers to see if they'd break the news to his family. I gather he has one?'

'Wife, and three kids all getting to an age where they've started to tangle with us, but nothing much at the moment – they've restricted their activities to shoplifting sweeties and breaking the windows of unoccupied houses.'

'I think I'll ask Teri Friend. She's good with empathising and looking after weeping women. Me, I just freeze and can't say a word.'

'Me too,' agreed Monty, who hated strong emotions, and was very happy safely ensconced in his lair of records. He was still in the process of adding some of the earlier ones to the hated computer, while doggedly maintaining his own paper system.

Lenny left him to his routine record updating and went off in search of Teri Friend. She might feel that breaking bad news was rather beneath her level of experience in the job, but experience gave you tact and taught you the best way to tackle difficult and sensitive jobs like this one.

From the vestibule, before the door closed properly, he heard Teri's voice saying, 'Not *another* racial minority case? My Asian roots don't qualify me as an authority on racial matters, you know.'

'That's not the case, love,' answered Lenny. 'Just something a bit sensitive: telling a woman her husband's been murdered in a very unusual and cruel way.'

Over her time in the job Teri had got used to older officers like Lenny addressing her as 'love', and she had no real objection unless there was a senior officer lurking in the background. She smiled at him and said, 'Thanks a bleedin' bunch, Lenny, that makes me the bad news budgie again. Give me the address and the details, and I'll get it over with before I rebel and insist that you do it for once.'

'Hold on there, love. I'd never be able to be as good as you are at doing this sort of thing, and you know it.'

'Oh, don't I, and in spades!'

CHAPTER SIX

Olivia and Hal went back into the hospital about three o'clock. There'd have to be some open and honest talking when Ben came home, to get to the bottom of why this incident had occurred in the first place. She would never erase the memory of a medic shaking her son's inert body and shouting, 'Breathe!'

In the car on the drive over, Olivia had asked her husband why he'd suddenly decided to go into the bedroom. It turned out that Hal had gone into the upstairs bathroom and seen that somebody had taken a crap on the carpet, having completely missed the bowl of the lavatory. He had known that it was either Ben or his friend who had done such a filthy thing, and had marched straight to the horse's mouth (or, rather, its arse) to demand an explanation. He had found the friend gone and Ben barely conscious.

'Well, he's never seeing that lad again. He's obviously trouble, although I thought he was so well-spoken, and he had a good address,' commented Olivia.

'A nice accent and good address are no indication of character though, are they, Liv? If his mother's place is stuffed with Valium and old-fashioned sleeping pills there must be something wrong in the household,' countered Hal.

'We have sleeping pills in our medicine cabinet,' Olivia rounded on him.

'We do indeed, but they were left by your mother on her last visit to us before she fell off her perch. They're probably wildly out of date, and work more by luck than efficacy.'

'We could send him over to visit your parents?'

'You've got to be joking. The last thing we need is for him to be left to his own devices on an island that isn't unknown for its supply of marijuana.'

'God, I didn't even think of that. Well, we'll have to do something.'

'Not until we've talked it over with him. Remember, we've got to start treating him as an adult if he wants to be viewed as one.'

Ben was awake and gave them a weak smile when he saw them come through the doorway of his room. 'I kinda screwed up badly, didn't I?' he asked weakly.

Olivia immediately rushed to his bed, unable to contain her sobbing, and threw her arms round him, just grateful to see that he didn't seem to be suffering from any long-term damage after his close brush with death.

Hal walked over more slowly, tears of gratitude rolling down his cheeks. Olivia moved away slightly, and Hal took Ben's light brown face in his large dark brown hands. He leaned over and kissed his son's forehead with a tenderness that belied his size. 'My son,' was all he said, repeating it several times before he took his palms from the boy's cheeks.

DS Groves had had more than enough to distract her mind from her chaotic and catastrophic domestic situation that day, and when she could delay going home no longer, she packed up, put on her fiercest expression of determination, and headed for Home Farm Barn. Things couldn't be allowed to fall into any pattern other than one of her own devising.

Although her hands shook on the steering wheel as she drove, she found that when she approached the front door, she was icily calm. Fortunately her key still let her in, and she went into the house calling out to Kenneth so that they could talk this situation out. She had phoned her solicitor that afternoon and asked him to start divorce proceedings, and she knew exactly what she wanted, domestically.

Kenneth looked a bit grey about the gills and sheepish without the wine inside him and the bravado of the night before with which it had imbued him, and Gerda looked half triumphant, half scared.

Gathering her courage, like scattered troops, Lauren glared as fiercely as she could and said, 'Right! This needs sorting, and it needs sorting now. You, Kenneth' – she pointed at him – 'are hardly ever here, so I suggest that you move into the granny annexe while you are. That will keep me where I need to be for contacts from work and postage et cetera, and when the children are here, it's easy access for you.

'I shall live in the main house. And you' – she pointed to Gerda – 'can get out of here. Pack your bags and bugger off. I know you'll understand that expression because your English is so very good.'

At this point she was interrupted by Kenneth. 'Gerda's going nowhere,' he announced. 'I'll bow to your wish to move into the annexe, but Gerda comes with me, and when I go away again she'll be coming with me too. You haven't fired her; she simply doesn't work for you anymore. She and I will be living together.'

'Well, you'd better not try to get the house or the children,' said Lauren anxiously. 'I've already spoken to my solicitor and explained the situation to him, asking him to initiate divorce proceedings on the grounds of your infidelity.'

'That's fine by me, Lauren, as long as I get access to my children. When we,' – he indicated Gerda, who had slunk up to his side – 'have some of our own, however, I may need to seek to have the house sold to be divided equally between us. I shall need a family home for any future children.'

Lauren was speechless with a mixture of disbelief and shock. Had Kenneth really thought this far ahead? Had he been planning for this to happen for a long time already? Fetching the key for the door to the little apartment that lay beyond the walls of the utility room, she handed it to her now estranged husband and marched into the sitting room to read her latest eBook, for she certainly didn't want to be around when Kenneth and his harlot packed and they moved next door together.

She found her throat was constricted with grief at this sudden turnaround, even though she realised that she didn't love Kenneth anymore, and Gerda was welcome to him and his animal lusts and lack of empathy. Kenneth loved Kenneth and money, in that order. At least he was assured of always earning plenty of the latter.

Klaxons and alarms were going off, Olivia shouting and screaming, 'Do something! For God's sake do something, somebody!' Hal was paralysed with shock, moaning softly to himself the words of the Lord's Prayer. White-coated people were rushing hither and thither until the moment when the one in authority asked everyone to stand back from the bed, placed the two paddles on Ben's chest and shouted, 'Clear!', the boy's body arcing as the current went through him.

Lauren could stand the evening no longer, and took herself out of the house just to get away from the over-loud laughing and giggling that was going on behind the door to the annexe. It was obviously an act put on for her benefit, and she wouldn't grace them with her presence and discomfort any longer. She'd leave quietly, though, so that they carried on with the strain of their forced gaiety for as long as possible before they realised she'd gone.

She grabbed the weekend holdall she had used so shortly before, and drove off to the Hardys' cottage, hoping to get news of Ben and offload some of her own troubles at the same time – after all, that was what she'd gone over for the night before.

When she pulled into the narrow driveway, she could see that Olivia and Hal were just getting out of a car and approaching the house, Olivia in floods of tears, Hal's face pale and stern. Tentatively getting out of her own car, she approached them calling, 'Is everything all right' but with a feeling in her stomach that nothing was right at all.

Back at Littleton-on-Sea Police Station, Sergeant Penny Sutcliffe had resumed her usual place on the reception desk after a day's leave, taking no time at all to make the place her lair again, and removing all signs of her temporary replacement.

She was a married woman with three children, and had spurned any further promotions or offers of plainclothes work to retain the predictability of her shift work. She had no desire or need for unsocial hours without any warning, nor for working all night. There were two other regular shift desk sergeants to take her place when she wasn't on duty, and they kept their own places for things, without interfering with the working practices of the other.

Having been freed up from the reception desk, Teri Friend joined the group of officers who were putting in a lot of unpaid overtime to find out as much as they could about their two savagely murdered victims. She had been paired with Liam Shuttleworth to execute door-to-door enquiries along the last houses in front of the beach, and also putting up incident signs asking for any witnesses to contact the police if they thought they had seen anything suspicious.

· Colin Redwood was searching as rapidly as possible through their computer records looking for anyone who might be involved in the local drugs culture, whether as dealer or client, and Lenny Franklin was in the archives with Monty Fairbanks, doing the same thing with the computer that was Monty's brain, and his little pieces of card. If they could, between them, they would assemble a suspect list, for this was so obviously to do with drugs, both victims having been full of them, that the answers must lie with this particular slice of the dark underbelly of the town.

Superintendent Devenish had chivvied along the press officer and demanded that he be allowed a radio and television appeal about both deaths, and these had duly been broadcast. He hadn't given details of the actual murder methods, but had appealed for anyone who had anything suspicious to report, or unexplained, that might be able to further their enquiries – then appealed, somewhat hypocritically, that he would appreciate a blanket veto by the press on reporting the proceedings, in the interests of the ongoing investigations. He wormed his way round a few press questions at the end, then slipped off with all the acumen of an eel in a hurry.

He loved the media limelight, and had fussed like a prospective beauty queen before the mirror in his office before going to record the appeal. Proud as a peacock, vain as a top model, he did not recognise these failings in himself, and had therefore been confused when he saw officers tittering in corners when he made his way to the site of the recording.

Having had his shining hour, he looked into the CID office to make sure there was plenty of activity, being told that two officers were in the archives, then returned to his own office for a further primp and preen. While playing with a stray strand or two that had somehow escaped from his fairly hairless crown, he decided that he'd give the whole bunch of them a rocket tomorrow. It may not have been long since the bodies had been found, but the methods of murder had been so ghastly that he wanted no more such stains on his patch. He would like the whole thing wrapped up fast, his reputation unsullied.

By half past ten, Teri Friend and Liam Shuttleworth were back, having done all they could for the day and those working in the building had already assembled a fairly long list of suspects who were involved in, or on the periphery of, the drugs world, either with a record, or just a caution. The rounding-up and interviews would start the next day. Whoever was responsible for these two deaths needed catching and putting away for a very long time.

All the information and names gathered were put into a new file and left on the inspector's desk for the next day, provided she was coming in to work. If she failed to show again, they would either have to ask for another senior officer, or DS Groves would have to continue in the role, and she seemed too low a rank to be SIO in such a serious case.

Inside the Hardys' pretty cottage, three adults let tears roll freely. Olivia had been the first to speak her misery. 'He seemed to be all right – I mean, he was asleep when we went in this morning, but this afternoon he seemed to be awake and know who we were, and then he just went.

'The alarms went off, and he just lay there – there was nothing. A crash team came and worked on him, but it took them three shocks to get him back, then they took him off to intensive care. They put him into a coma that they wanted to keep him in for a couple of days, while he was on a ventilator and God knows what else. The doctor thought there must have been something else in that cocktail that he took, and which had attacked his heart as it reached its half-life, whatever that means.

'All I know is that he's in the ICU, he's seriously ill again, and that he's got to see a psychiatrist in case he tried to take his own life.'

'I can't take all this in,' growled Hal in his deep, rich voice, wiping tears from his eyes with the back of one of his huge hands.

'And even if they identify what else he took, there's no telling whether it could have done him permanent harm,' Olivia wailed in her misery of the unknown. 'What am I going to do if he's brain-damaged – or if he dies. I shall die, too, of grief. It must somehow be all our fault. It's all *my* fault. I should never have gone back to work full-time. I should've been home, here for him when he needed me, instead of chasing up the criminal activities of other people's kids.'

'Don't blame yourself, Liv,' said Hal, putting an arm around her. 'I retired and I'm here a lot for the time. That obviously hasn't helped at all. He just made a bad choice.'

'But we could lose him, and we've already lost all that time with him, not being here. You were the same when you taught, always tied up in lesson plans, evaluating students, marking work, and setting work. We hardly ever saw you. Our kids must have dragged themselves up like little orphans.'

Olivia was inconsolable, and Hal knew he had to intervene before she became hysterical. 'We did our best. We've been no different to most parents. We did what we could, when we could, and the best we could according to our circumstances. Some of the best-educated kids, the most supervised, go much further off the rails than this. It's one teenage over-indulgence in drugs. Don't get it out of proportion. There's a reason for this. All we've got to do is uncover it and try to put it right.'

'Hal, what if we lost him? I don't think I could bear it without him.'

'He'll come through it, you'll see. They're going to phone from the hospital when they've identified whatever other drugs he took, and they said we could go in in the morning to see him and get an update.'

At that particular moment, the telephone jangled, making all three of them jump. Olivia went off to answer it, half in hope that it was news of her darling son, and half in dread that the news would be bad.

They heard her end the call, then dial another number, having a second short conversation before returning to the other two, her eyes momentarily dry, her expression grim.

'What was it?' asked Hal hopefully. 'And who did you ring afterwards?'

'It was that bloody boy's junkie mother again. She said she's also noticed some of her travel sickness tablets have disappeared from the bedroom cabinet, and her son's owned up to taking them as well. She gave me the name of the active ingredient, and I've just called the information to the hospital so that they can get on with treating it. The nurse said she'd have to contact the poisons department in some London hospital to check on its full effects, but don't ask me which hospital, because it went in one ear and out of the other.'

'So what's happening?'

'She said someone would ring us back as soon as they knew the best treatment for whatever this bloody chemical is – hyoscine, I think she said – and give us an up-to-date prognosis.'

'They didn't know about this drug?'

'Apparently they didn't test for it because they thought it was such an unlikely ingredient in a cocktail to get high. Don't ask me – I'm not a bloody nurse. How the hell should I know?'

Hal stomped off to the kitchen and returned with a tray containing three glasses, and a bottle each of red and white wine. Removing a corkscrew from his pocket, he suggested that they drink the white first, and leave the red to breathe for at least five minutes before starting on it as their second course.

'This makes us no better than Ben, if we drink too much,' announced Olivia glumly. 'Alcohol's a drug as well, a poison that the body has to neutralise.'

'Do you want a drink or not?' asked Hal in a disgruntled voice.

'I'll have white,' she replied, all memory of her previous well-intentioned remark already erased from her memory. She needed a drink, and no amount of proselytising would wipe out that need.

'Would you like white, too?' Hal asked Lauren.

'No, I think I'd prefer black,' she said, then flushed furiously at her Freudian slip. She panicked as she realised it could be deemed to be unforgiveable.

Instead of seeming hurt or reproving, though, Hal suddenly burst into peals of delighted laughter, put down the bottle he was holding, and clutched at his stomach. 'That's brought us back down to earth. I presume that's a red for you then, Lauren?'

'Yes. I don't know how to apologise enough ...'

'Don't be silly. Do you think that's the first time that's happened to me? Would you like to consider my age and add it up?'

'If you're sure I haven't upset you ...'

'Lady, you've made my day. That's the first thing that's made me laugh since before I found Ben last night, and you have my undying thanks for that. So, what's gone wrong in your life? There must be something, as you dossed down here last night and came back this evening.'

Lauren found it easier to tell than she'd thought possible. 'I went home knowing I'd find Kenneth there, then I picked up some strange vibes and concluded that Gerda and Kenneth had been to bed together. When I went to her room to confront her, she said they'd been at it like knives since just after she started working for us, and we ... sort of had a fight. That's how I split my lip, when she pulled me to the floor.'

'Good God in Heaven, Lauren. Why didn't you say something?' Olivia was stunned at her friend and work partner's reticence in this matter.

'How could I, with everything that went off here. I couldn't say anything when I first got here because I felt ashamed, as if it were my fault somehow. Then Hal found Ben, and you know the rest.'

'But what's happened since? Have you been home since then?'

'I contacted my solicitor – actually, he's our solicitor, but I got first bagsy – and I've initiated divorce proceedings; gosh, how formal that sounds! When I got home tonight, I was about to give Kenneth the news that I was divorcing him when he floored me with the news that when he went back to work, he was taking Gerda with him, but he'd need use of the granny annexe for him *and her* when he was on leave, so that he could keep in contact with the kids. Then he had the cheek to inform me that when they had a family of their own, he'd need to sell the house, making his own kids homeless, so that he could house the little bastards he intends to father in the future.'

The two women grasped each other in a full body hug, and Hal put his arms around both of them. 'Oh, my poor injured darlings,' he crooned. 'You've both been through the wringer, haven't you, in the last twenty-four hours.'

Olivia suddenly broke away. 'Has anybody let Hibbie know? And where the hell is she anyway? And what happened in the office today? I haven't even given work a thought.'

Hal got in first. 'I texted her this morning, and she replied that she'd stay on where she was as it was convenient at the moment. I haven't let her know about this turn for the worse, because it could still all be a storm in a teacup.

'And we've got that other body,' said Lauren, 'but I don't want you to concern yourself about that now. We'll muddle through, somehow. We've both got messes to sort out, and life demands that they're what we concentrate on,' she declared. 'I'll call in for both of us tomorrow and speak to Superintendent Devenish, to see if we can both have a couple of days' compassionate leave.'

'But we can't …'

'That's what's going to happen, and there's no point in you arguing, guv. Neither of us would be any use on a major crime scene at the moment, so I think it's best left to someone who can concentrate all their mind on the finer points than let us two loose with all the distractions we have to live with for now. We'd be worse than a couple of rookie PCs.'

'But the other murder …'

'If you really want to know the details, I'll tell you after we've all had a couple of glasses more wine each, but it's unpleasant and I don't want to upset you anymore.'

'Nobody could achieve that at the moment. I just want to know.'

The next morning brought good news from the hospital. The additional substance had been checked and, thankfully, dealt with, and they were going to wake Ben that evening, if his parents wanted to come in when they took him off the ventilator. Olivia had been told in no uncertain terms by her sergeant that she had spoken to Devenish, and he would get some support staff in if they could be certain to come back the next day.

Not sure whether this would possible, but fairly certain it would be a good thing to get back to work as long as she could concentrate, Lauren went home to see what the situation was; whether she'd been relegated to the garden shed while the erstwhile au pair lorded it in her former bedroom, perhaps.

She was pleased to find that there was no other human presence in the house, and that, after a quick peek through the windows of the annexe, there seemed to be a lot of possessions thrown about in some disorder. Kenneth's car was gone from the garage, and she presumed that he and his paramour were still resident in the annexe, and that they had gone out together. That suited her fine.

They could stay there, thought Lauren, as she went up to Gerda's little apartment up in the attic and gathered up all the German woman's possessions, then dragged them all down to the annexe door. She pushed a note under the bottom of the door to inform them that she had returned all that was Gerda's, and that she hoped they'd be very happy together. And she meant it. Today, to use a shameless cliché, was the first day of the rest of her life.

She felt a shudder of shame run through her as her hope was tainted with poor Olivia's continuing uncertainty about the recovery of her son, but she didn't have the energy to worry about more than one person at the moment – and that person was her. She'd need to advertise for a holiday nanny and a cleaner, for when the children were home. Or, she could advertise for a live-in housekeeper, and choose her own candidate. She'd managed as practically a one-parent family for years now, and there seemed no reason why she couldn't do it permanently, with the necessary domestic help.

Back at the police station, Superintendent Devenish had decided to take things into his own hands rather than chasing after recently retired detectives to fill the unexpected absences of two of his plain clothes officers. He had been warned about promoting women in plain clothes, been told that they'd never stand the emotional strain or the call of domestic matters, but he didn't consider what Detective Sergeant Groves had told him in confidence that morning as anything like that.

Both Groves and DI Hardy had suffered domestic disasters that would equally have made his male detectives take at least a few days off work, and he had no criticism of them requesting some compassionate leave. Devenish had decided to take over the investigation himself, an unprecedented move but one designed to keep everything in-house. He warned his staff, nonetheless, that he didn't want his involvement bandied about, during his morning briefing on what had been squirrelled out of their records the previous evening by 'a bunch of dedicated officers who gave up their own time out of devotion to duty', everyone knowing that he was making clear that the overtime budget had already been blown for the month.

House-to-house enquiries would continue near both sites, and known offenders would be brought in for questioning – a long and laborious process which might yield precisely nothing, but which would nevertheless have to be done.

'I have every faith in your abilities, and I would be delighted to see these two unfortunate matters cleared up as quickly as possible,' he told them, while at the same time realising that it was very unlikely to happen.

INTERLUDE

'Good job so far, lads. I think we've earned ourselves a takeaway, don't you?'

There was a rowdy cheer at this suggestion, and they all headed for one of the pubs down near the river, where there was usually dance music playing, live or piped. The rounds were simple – four pints of lager and four whisky chasers – and there were three rounds.

As the last one was put on the table, the main man said, 'I think we'll have that one over there in the pink glitter. What do you think, eh?'

'Looks absolutely delicious. Can we all have the same?'

'I don't see why not?'

'Will we put the container in the bin afterwards? I think so. There's a big black one just at the back of the pub. We should be able to put it in that when all the punters have gone and the landlord's safely tucked up in bed for the night. I'll go and place our order, shall I, and meet you outside. Same as always, except we'll clear up after ourselves this time.'

The man who had spoken rose and approached a girl at the bar sipping cider through a straw, braving out any lusty glances towards her through her thick covering of make-up.

'Hello there, love. Would you like another drink? Only I'm going to have one, and I want to play a trick on my mates, if you wouldn't mind coming outside with me for a minute. There's a score in it for you. Easy money, and I'll order when we get back in.'

The young, over-painted face turned up to him and smiled, and she went with him without a murmur, at the promise of twenty quid and a free drink.

CHAPTER SEVEN

As Kenneth wasn't due to go back to the Middle East for another three days, Lauren was at her desk by 7.30 the next morning. She didn't really want to be in the kitchen when those two started larking around in the annexe right next door – something she suspected they might do purely to get at her. She had to catch up with rapidly developing events in the murder case anyway. The case would obviously go to Olivia now, and she needed to get a grip on what she'd missed, as she had been acting SIO when the most recent murder victim had been discovered. She needed to hand over to her boss with as much detail as she could.

There had been a lot of interview and door-to-door enquiries reports left on her desk, and she set to going through them all, making her own notes. She felt Olivia would be in good spirits when she arrived. Lauren had been relieved when the DI had phoned her, just after six in the hope that she'd be up, to inform her that the hospital had just called. Ben had had a comfortable night after they'd left the previous evening, and was in no further need of the ventilator. His heart also seemed to be behaving itself too.

The DI intended to go into the hospital on the way to work, and would leave Hal with him, on guard. She would be in at her normal time, and she didn't want news of what was going on getting round the station grapevine; they'd twist it all sorts of ways and she'd never live it down. Rumour seemed to be believed more avidly than truth.

When the DI did arrive, she breezed into the office

trying to look as normal as possible, as if she'd just spent her two days off at her leisure, and greeted everyone as she made for her desk. Her desk was positioned opposite Lauren's, with her back to the DCs, and, just for a few seconds after she had sat down she let her face relax into an expression more akin to what she really felt like inside.

Lauren had the good luck to be looking her way at that moment, and cast her a questioning glance. Discreetly and out of sight of the others, Olivia gave her the thumbs-up to indicate that Ben's condition had not worsened, then began trying to sort through the paperwork that had appeared on her desk in the previous two days. Much of it was superfluous to current enquiries, a lot of it general internal stuff that she could ignore for now. When she had sorted the wheat from the chaff, she summoned her sergeant to the other side of her desk with a nod of the head, and asked her to go through everything they had so far.

As many officers as could be spared had been engaged in enquiries, trying to identify individuals and locations involved in drugs, and several known faces had been brought in for questioning. Indeed, the cells were fully occupied at the moment with a few who had been picked up very early this morning, before they could be up and about.

The last four still to be interviewed were Teddy Edwards, aka Woggle-Eye; Steve Stoner, aka Flinty; Mervyn Lord, aka The Knife; and Dennis Trussler, aka Scabby. Lauren looked at her superior, expecting information on these peculiarly named characters. Being fairly new to the town, she hadn't come across these individuals before.

'They're a right bad lot,' Hardy explained. 'Drugs, mugging; aggravated burglary; shoplifting; ABH – GBH for Trussler; illegal dog fighting; D&D; driving while under the influence; assaulting a police officer; resisting arrest; and TWOCing.

'They've done just about everything except being nailed for a long stint in jail, and they've escaped CPS charges on several occasions because of lack of physical evidence or witnesses suddenly changing their stories. I suppose we'd better include intimidating witnesses in that list as well, because that wouldn't surprise me at all. And that's just what we know about. God knows what else they've got up to undetected.

'All four of them have been known to the police since they were pre-teens, and none of them seems to understand the concept of going straight. I don't think any of them have ever worked a day in their lives.' 'They sound a right bunch. Are they fairly young?' asked Lauren, innocently.

'A bit of a mix really. Trussler is in his forties, Lord isn't far behind, but the other two are only in their twenties and look up to the other two as sort of godfather characters.'

'But they've all been in prison?'

'Yes, but not for nearly long enough, and not for anywhere near enough of their crimes.'

'Can we interview them together, or would you rather one of the men went in with you?' asked the sergeant, hoping to get the chance to have a peek at these local villains.

'What, go in with one of those pussies? You've got to be kidding. No, I'd rather have you by my side.'

'Shall we start now?'

'No time like the present, Groves.'

The first detainee brought in was Woggle-Eye Edwards, who had suffered an overdose of some unknown substance years ago, and had been left with a wandering eye. He was twenty-nine years old, and as vicious as an American pitbull. He had insisted that his 'brief' was present when he was interviewed, and a solicitor sat in with him on the other side of the table.

Edwards had a shaven head covered in tattoos, and some disturbingly large holes in the lobes of his ears. His nose also sported several gold rings. Compounded by his grey and irregular teeth, he was a most unprepossessing character, someone who was regularly avoided in the street by less exotic members of the public.

Lauren had the times of death estimated by the pathologist in her notebook and, after Hardy had started the tape, took heed of her nod and asked their 'guest' where he had been at the times of both of the killings.

'No comment,' he stated with a smirk and what could have been a sideways glance at his brief, but which could just have been a spasm in his mismatched eyes.

Olivia immediately interrupted. 'Don't start with the "no comment" routine. I've had my fill of that off you over the years, Edwards. Give us some answers that we can check out, or I'll keep you in custody until the awful tea in here loosens your tongue for you.'

'Are you going to beat me, Inspector? Ooh, I'm so frightened,' he concluded in a falsetto voice.

'Only at chess, you muppet. Now, be a good boy and tell us where you were at the times given to you by DS Groves here.'

Edwards assumed what was, for him, a thoughtful expression, but which appeared more like a threatening grimace. Eventually he reluctantly said, 'I was wiv me mates. They'll tell you that's where I was.'

'And which mates would these be?'

'Flinty, The Knife, and Scabby. We was all together. They'll back me on that.'

'I bet they will. And just where were you all four together so conveniently?'

'Dunno.'

'You don't know where you were, or you were somewhere you didn't recognise.'

'Can't remember. I was off me face.'

Hardy sighed before continuing, 'Was it just the four of you, or were there other people who could have seen you?'

'Can't remember. I told ya, I was off me face.'

'What on?'

'The floor, I fink.'

'Very funny. Did you have anything to do with the deaths of Richard Dunbar or Douglas Green?'

'Never 'eard of 'em.'

'Please look at these photographs and tell me if you recognise the men in them. For the benefit of the tape I am handing *Mr* Edwards photographs of the two murder victims.'

Edwards tossed the photos on to the table with a sneer. 'Never seen either of them before in me life,' he replied.

As the photographs hit the top of the desk the door opened soundlessly to let in DC Colin Redwood, a grim expression on his face. He approached Hardy and whispered in her ear before leaving the room. 'Interview terminated at ...' Hardy wound up the proceedings and asked that Mr Edwards be returned to his quarters. Edwards looked stunned and said in disbelief, 'Aren't you letting me go, then?'

'Not on your life, sunshine. You're as guilty as hell about something, and I intend to get to the bottom of what it is. You were lying through your crooked teeth the whole time we were being recorded ...'

She didn't get any further, as the solicitor interrupted, saying that he didn't like her manner towards his client. Woggle-Eye gave a superior smirk, though it disappeared from his face soon enough when he was escorted back to his cell to await further questioning.

As Groves trotted along behind the bustling tubby figure of Hardy, she asked what had come up, and why they were rushing.

'A young girl, Genni Lacey, has gone missing. Didn't come home last night, and her parents thought she might be staying with a friend. Even though her mobile was going straight to voicemail, they didn't worry too much. It was only when she didn't come back this morning, either, that they phoned some of her friends and it was then they realised there was something wrong. When the friends all came back and said they hadn't seen her, the mother phoned her in as a missing person. A missing minor: she's only fourteen years old.'

'So we're going to interview the parents, are we?'

'While Uniform searches the house and garden.'

'Shouldn't we carry on with the interviews, though? After all, two men are dead, boss.'

'Yes, and they'll be just as dead whether or not we take time off to speak to the distressed parents of the missing girl. *She* might still be alive, and our investigating at this stage could make all the difference.'

'Message received and understood, Inspector. Why didn't I think of that?'

'Because you're not a hard-nosed bitch like me,' replied Hardy, who then had to blow said nose rather theatrically as the thought of her Ben still lying in the hospital came to mind. 'I'll tell you what, I'll get Colin Redwood and Lenny to have a go at them all, and we can listen to the tapes later. Colin's really straining at the leash at the moment and Lenny's seen everything there is to see. He's as likely to be intimidated as an egg is to fry in a freezer.'

'That sounds like a good idea, guv.'

'It certainly sounds like one to me. I look forward to the results.'

'So what exactly are we going to do?'

'If there's no trace found of Genni at the house, we can try to reconstruct her last known movements, who last saw her, that sort of thing, then we can get a search party organised. No doubt devilish Devenish would like to spruce himself up again for a public appeal.'

'I hate it when the homes of missing kids are searched, as if their parents are suspected of killing them and concealing the body,' Lauren said.

'But how often that turns out to be true,' said Olivia.

The girl's family home turned out to be on a new estate of four and five-bedroomed houses. Although the estate was on the very outskirts of the town and the last houses had only recently been sold, already new building was extending further into the countryside. The structures of smaller houses had sprung up beyond the estate like wooden-framed saplings, and there seemed to be no end to the relentless march into what had all been fields when Olivia was young.

They didn't reach the doorbell to ring it, as the front door was opened to them as soon as they started up the path by a weeping woman with red eyes and a slumped-over posture. She was about forty, and looked as if she usually dressed smartly, but couldn't quite carry it off today. Her cardigan was buttoned wrongly, her tights laddered, and her hair unsprayed and flying away from what was probably its normally immaculate coiffure.

Behind her was a man of similar age, dressed as if for the office in a suit, white shirt, and tie, but wearing the expression of one who did not want to change into something more informal in case it was bad luck. As they were bidden to enter, a marked car pulled up by the kerb containing the uniformed officers who would conduct the search of the property. They were in luck with it being a modern structure: there were so many less nooks and crannies in which to conceal a body; not that they expected to find one.

Thomas Lacey, the missing girl's father, directed the uniformed officers towards the attic, where they would start searching the house from the top down, while the girl's mother, Abi, showed the two detectives into a minimalist and spacious living room, referred to, rather horribly in Lauren's opinion, as 'the lounge'.

When all were seated on the comfortable white leather suite, Mrs Lacey asked them if they had any news of their Genni. She seemed to check herself, before adding that the girl's full name was Imogen, but they had shortened this to Genni, spelling it out for Lauren, who was taking notes oblivious to the fact that Olivia had already brought out her voice-activated recorder and received a nod of confirmation from the parents that it was all right to use it.

'When did you last see your, er, Genni?' asked Hardy, trying to look as sympathetic as possible. She had had a case like this about five years ago, when a little boy had gone missing, and his body had turned up shoved behind the panel of the bath – although it must have been moved there after the police search, for he wasn't there when they had carried it out. The parents had later confessed that his body had been in a suitcase in the overhead beams of the garage, and the officers must have missed this on their search of the property. And they had seemed such concerned parents, too, worried almost out of their wits – and it had all turned out to be a con.

It was Mrs Lacey who spoke. 'She went out yesterday just after she'd eaten her tea. She always has something when she comes in from school, and we eat later on, when Thomas is home from work.'

'So did you see her then, Mr Lacey?'

'No, I haven't seen her since I dropped her off at school yesterday morning.' That would need checking, thought Hardy, to see that she actually had reached school, and that the mother wasn't just covering up for her husband.

'Let's get some basics sorted out first,' Hardy had requested. 'How old is Genni, and have you got a recent photograph of her that we can use in our search?'

'She'll be fifteen in three weeks' time, and I've got her most recent school photograph on the wall unit. I *will* get it back, won't I?'

'Of course you will, Mrs Lacey. What did your daughter do when she had finished her meal?'

'She went upstairs for a while, then she came down in a T-shirt and jeans and with her rucksack. She told me she was off to a friend's house, and that she'd be back at bedtime.'

'And that was all right, was it?'

'She had her mobile phone. We thought that if she could call us and we could check with her, then she'd be fine.'

'We usually advise parents of young teenagers, especially girls, to ask them for a contact landline number for where they're going, so that it can be checked that they've arrived, then get the child to phone the parents either for a lift home if it's after dark, or to tell them that they'll be home within a short time-frame.'

Both parents looked devastated, and Lauren felt that she had to say something. 'We do realise that it's very easy to be wise after the event, and if you've always been able to trust your child before, you might not have seen the necessity to take precautions like that.'

'What did your daughter eat for her tea before she went out?' asked Hardy, trying not to be affected by what seemed genuine panic on the parents' faces.

'Why do you want to …? Oh my God, you think she's dead, don't you? You think she's dead, and you're just not telling us.' Abi's face was as white as paper as she said this, her voice shrill and panicked, and Thomas went over and sat beside her, an arm around her shoulders, his hand pulling her head down to rest on him.

'There, there, Abi, love,' he comforted her. 'She'll have lost her phone and gone off somewhere without a thought for all the worry she's causing.'

Pulling herself away from her husband, she said, 'But she's not that kind of girl at all. She's always meticulous about telling us where she's going.'

'And do you often check?' asked Hardy, giving them a hard look.

'No, we don't. Up until now we've always trusted her.'

Hardy remained silent, letting them work it out for themselves. 'You mean she could have been up to anything, don't you, and we'd have been none the wiser?' Abi whispered.

'To be honest, that's about the size of it, Mrs Lacey,' replied the inspector, hard but truthful.

'Oh, God, Thomas, whatever are we going to do?'

'What you need to do,' Hardy advised them, 'is to stay calm and answer our questions. So, what did she have for tea before she went out?'

'She just had a slice of pizza and a cup of tea, she has a full meal at school,' answered Mrs Lacey.

'Now, I want you to go through her wardrobe and tell me if any of her clothes are missing.'

'But she was dressed in jeans when she went out. Oh, do you think she might have run away? But why? I can't think of any reason. I mean, the three of us always get on very well.'

'She had her rucksack with her when she went. She could have had anything in that. Just check for me, please, so that we can assure ourselves that that probably hasn't happened. Please.'

'I'll go, Thomas,' said Mrs Lacey. 'I know what she's got and where she keeps it.' She passed the searching uniformed officers on the landing, on their way downstairs to examine the ground floor, the garden and garage; garden sheds and shelters would not be exempt from their prying hands and eyes, either.

Entering the first bedroom on the right, Mrs Lacey opened the door and said, 'This is Genni's room. Where shall I start?'

INTERLUDE – FLASHBACK

The girl reached a woozy consciousness sufficient to inform her that her legs were bound at the ankles, her tied wrists behind her back. It was dark wherever she was, but she was lying on a very hard floor and the place smelled terrible. She had no memory of the night before, not after entering the pub and showing her fake ID, and had no idea how she could have got here, or why; or, for that matter, who would have put her here and bound her hand and foot.

One of the last things she noticed was that her knickers were gone and that her already short shirt was round her thighs. She felt a pain between her legs, and had the sinking feeling that something terrible had happened to her. She'd only gone to the pub last night for a dare and, when she got home, she was going to ring the members of her little gang and tell them what she'd done.

Tears stung her eyes as she was overcome by a wave of self-pity. Why weren't her parents here to rescue her? Then she realised that not only had she never told them where she was really going, she didn't even have any idea how much time had passed since she went into the pub.

If her hands hadn't been bound, she'd phone them, and maybe they could get the signal traced, but a quick wriggle around revealed the fact that her phone was no longer in the pocket of her jacket. Although this was undone, as was her blouse, she could make out that there was unlikely to be anything in her pockets at all. They felt completely empty. Maybe there would be other people nearby, and she'd just been left here until somebody stumbled upon her. She took a deep breath and called for help.

Within a few seconds of her voice echoing around the confines of the building, a metal door grated against the floor nearby, and she knew she wasn't alone any more. She felt paralysed with fear. Whoever had taken her didn't seem to have deserted her at all. She could hear footsteps in the darkness and the sound of voices whispering, feet descending metal stairs then crossing the concrete towards her.

'There she is, fresh as a daisy, and just ready for round two. Ready, lads? Put the light on, for fuck's sake. How are we going to be able to enjoy ourselves if we can't see her?

A bare lightbulb was illuminated high above her from a metal ceiling, and she saw four men surrounding her, each face wearing an evil leer. 'What are you going to do to me?' she squeaked, her voice high and hoarse at the same time. Only then did she realise how dry her mouth was, and how sore her throat.

'We're gonna show you a good time, little darlin'' said one of them, reaching down to fondle one of her budding breasts.

'Stop that. I don't like it,' she shouted, this time even more croakily, fear thrumming through her body like an electric current.

'You can scream as much as you like, sweetie. Nobody's gonna hear you out here. Right, get her clothes off.' At this point she thought they were at least going to untie her, but instead, someone took a wicked looking knife out of his jacket pocket and bent down to cut her clothes away from the front of her upper body.

Another one of them had removed a hypodermic needle from somewhere and was approaching her, while one of the others rolled her on to her side to expose the veins of one arm.

'No,' she screamed, wriggling in a desperate attempt to

get away from these monsters.

'Stop!' shouted a voice. 'Do we really need to do the first one with the volume down? Let's have this one with the sound up. Get her legs undone and weight them down, so we can get them apart. I want to see her face as she realises what a good time we're giving her. She ought to know what a lucky girl she is.'

As the ties were removed from her ankles she felt urine leaving her body in her distress. This was no bad dream. This was no practical joke. This was real, and worse things than this were about to happen to her.

'We can't risk it. Sorry, lads, but you know the rules on takeaways. The one with the hypodermic advanced once more, she felt a sharp prick to the inside of her right elbow, and the coldness of fluid entering the warmth of her vein ... then she knew no more as her struggling body slumped to complete immobility. She had just gone through the last goodnight without even a murmur.

CHAPTER EIGHT

'I don't understand it,' wailed Abi. 'What are these clothes doing in her wardrobe? They look like a hooker's clothes.'

'How often do you go into her wardrobe, Mrs Lacey?'

'Well … never. She always insists that she puts away her own clothes, so I just leave them on the bed for her when I've washed and ironed them. I've never seen any of *these* clothes before.'

'Would you mind looking in her drawers too, please,' asked Olivia, although she knew that if there was anything odd about their contents, the uniformed officers would have made a note of it.

A top drawer in the dressing table held a collection of bright make-up. Green and mauve eyeshadows vied for space with hot pink, orange, and red lipsticks, and there were false eyelashes and several mascara wands. Foundation, powder and blusher completed this find, along with a couple of kohl pencils. Nestling in the underwear drawer had also been a spray bottle of what Mrs Lacey had referred to as 'tarty perfume', and an opened packet of condoms with one missing.

'What the hell has my little girl been bullied into?' This was a typical reaction – the denial that their daughter, nearly fifteen, would have obtained anything like this of her own accord, and the disbelief that she was growing up and that these were things that they should have discussed with her. Many parents seemed to believe in a perpetual innocence for their children, not understanding that there could be all sorts of monkey business going on under an outwardly calm surface.

This was beginning to look very nasty, thought Hardy. 'I shall need addresses and/or contact numbers for her closest friends. Has she got a Facebook account and, if so, can we have a look at it?' the inspector asked, noticing a tiny table in the window that held a laptop.

Wandering over to it, she asked casually, 'Do you know your daughter's password for this?'

'Absolutely not,' replied Abi. 'This is totally private to her, and she won't let us anywhere near her when she's on it.'

'Do you mind if we take this away for examination?' It was less of a request than an order, but worded politely, and an answer in the negative would have been immediately overruled. Hardy was convinced that the computer held the answer to what Genni had been up to the night before, and the sooner they could get it to the station, the sooner the files could be accessed, especially her Facebook page. They could usually learn an awful lot from that. People seemed to see what they wrote in there as sacred, like writing in a locked diary would have been in the fifties.

'And she's definitely got her mobile on her, has she?'

'I've been ringing and ringing, and I just get sent to voicemail. I'll try one more time, but it won't make any difference. She saw it as some sort of protection – something that would keep her safe whatever – friends at the push of a button whenever she needed anything.'

Lauren put the laptop into a large evidence bag and, after a few more questions, they took their leave, pinning all their faith on the computer. If they could get into that they'd have all they needed on what she and her friends were talking about and perhaps discover what she was planning to do. It was surprising what a bunch of teenagers who chatted on Facebook would say, thinking naively that everything they said was private.

The Uniforms' search had produced no clues as to

where the young girl had gone but, thankfully, it hadn't revealed a hastily stowed body either.

Catching a quick lunch in the cafe next to the station where the coffee was more than drinkable, Hardy made a quick call to Hal to see how Ben was. Fortunately, Hal was somewhere where he didn't have to turn off the phone, and gave her an update. The boy was doing well, but hadn't reacted well to the visit from a shrink. The story their son told didn't seem possible, but Hal said they'd discuss it later when they were both home. Promising to ring back when he'd been in again during the afternoon, he left his wife to it, knowing she had important enquiries on hand.

Putting the phone back into her pocket, Olivia asked Lauren how things were at home. The younger woman's face immediately fell. She had, for a while, been able to refocus her mind onto the case from her domestic crisis, and now it all came flooding back to her.

'Kenneth's going back to the Middle East in a couple of days, and he's taking *her* with him. He says they're going to live together out there, and he'd like them to have use of the annexe when they come back on leave, so he can stay in close contact with the children.'

'He's really taking the au pair to the Middle East? It wasn't just bravado?' Olivia was astounded.

'So he says, and he said that we'd have to sort out selling the house so that he's got enough capital to purchase the property they'll need when they've got kids – but I've already told you all this. I'm afraid I'm rambling.'

'As I said, he can't do that!' Olivia said, horrified.

'Don't you worry about that. I've spoken to the solicitor, and he says he can delay any sale of the property until the youngest is through university. Kenneth might get what he wants but it's going to be a long time in the future, and in the meantime, he'll just have to manage with what he's already got. We're going nowhere, and he can't make us.'

'Good for you. I bet you'll be glad when they've both cleared off.'

'I certainly will,' replied the sergeant, staring into her cup sightlessly. She knew she had to get a grip on herself, as talking about the situation threatened her outward calm. She didn't want to find herself bawling her eyes out in a café and be unable to go back to work after lunch. There was simply too much to do, especially after Genni Lacey's disappearance.

Olivia felt rather the same, after the emotional strain and stress she and Hal had been through over the last couple of days, and there were still tricky days to come, when Ben was home recuperating. Would he be willing to talk the situation through with them like an adult? Would he be willing to accompany her on a visit to the rehab centre, where he could see the harm that drugs could do, or would he want to sweep everything under the carpet as if nothing had happened? The latter was the more likely, she felt, given his personality.

Changing the subject slightly, she asked Lauren what she was going to do about the children's schooling, as keeping up the fees for private school was surely going to be too expensive.

'I'm not going to fight Kenneth if he decides to take them out. There's a village school not far from us, just outside Littleton-on-Sea, and it has a good reputation. It fought off closure just last academic year due to falling numbers, so I'm sure the head would be delighted to gain two more pupils. Then I don't have to worry until they're eleven.

'I know there's still the eleven-plus exam round here, and a grammar school within reach, and I'm sure they're both bright enough to get through. It may not be the way I was educated, but it will probably be the best alternative to what I did have planned for them – and I would see a lot more of them. If I can be as good an example as Nanny and my parents were to me, I'm sure they'll turn out all right.

'The truth is, Olivia, I simply don't know yet. If I am allowed to stay in the house for as long as I want, he might decide that he needs the school fees money towards his cosy little love nest. I'll just have to try to achieve the best outcome that I can.'

'You'll carry on working, of course.' It was a statement rather than a question.

'I'll have to, but I can always replace Gerda with a childminder and a cleaner which, even together, will cost a lot less than that little slut. I'm capable of looking after my own home and children, given a little help. I can see no reason why I should have to give up my career for the want of some domestic support. It was interrupted for long enough after I had the children. I don't want to have to walk away from all the effort I've put in so far just because Kenneth can't keep his dick in his trousers.'

'Lauren!'

'Well. That's how I feel. It's the old one-eyed trouser-snake again, and we know that *they've* been the cause of trouble since the Garden of Eden. Anyway, are you going in to see Ben after work?'

'Yes, of course I am.

'I wondered if I could come with you.'

'Why?'

'Just for some friendly support.'

'Well, in that case, why don't you come home with me for a bite to eat after we've been there? Hal's band's playing tonight, and we could go and listen to him, maybe have a few drinks, listen to the music and catch a little distraction from all our worries, both personal and professional.'

'Olivia, you're a brick. I just need to get through the next couple of days. Whenever they know I'm in, those two go into an adolescent routine of canoodling very loudly, usually just the other side of the annexe entrance, and I'm heartily sick of it.'

'It's a date then. But we'd better get back and set some wheels in motion so that things don't stagnate. We may not be intending to work through the night, but there's no reason we can't get the press officer to set up a public appeal and get a search party out. We can appeal to volunteers from the public to go through all the derelict buildings down by the river, and what's left of the woods and agricultural land beyond the new developments. After all, she lived on one of those new estates. There's nothing to say that she didn't go missing from quite near home.'

The television appeal was arranged for the six o'clock regional news, with Abi and Thomas Lacey in attendance. For the rest of the afternoon, Groves and Hardy carried on the interviewing of the detainees they had had to abandon that morning. By the end of the working day they had learnt precisely nothing from their suspects, who were all well-versed in the culture of 'no comment', but a police search was underway, and some officers had been diverted to the green in front of the promenade to wait for volunteers from the public to join them.

The two detectives headed out to the hospital to visit Ben before returning to the Hardys' cottage, leaving the lovebirds at the barn conversion to wonder where their usual audience had sloped off to.

When they got back to the cottage, Hal had cooked up peas and rice with some of the goat meat he was able to get from an ethnic supermarket now, and they all ate heartily.

'If you want to come in early with me, Leon's coming over in the old bus. If we all go together with the band, we could all have a drink, and not have to worry about driving,' he suggested as they were forking food eagerly into their mouths.

'Get that man to open a bottle of wine,' declared Olivia, feeling that the relaxation from a few glasses of the grape would definitely help to chase away the blues.

'Hey, we is on de toot, tonight,' Hal answered, with a smile that included both of them. Just the thought of opening a bottle made the big man look slightly less strained.

It was good to get away from both home and the station, but Olivia found her eyes drawn constantly towards the bar. It was where Hal, on his last gig here, had suspected illegal drugs might be being sold. There were two girls and a young man serving, and for quite a while all seemed innocent enough, but as the time wore on, she just happened to turn her head and saw what she thought was definitely a dodgy deal going on.

The young barman looked both ways to see if he was being watched, at which point he dipped his gaze, then leaned over the bar and appeared to shake hands with one of the customers. The customer then put his hand in his pocket, as did the barman. There was definitely something to investigate there, in her opinion, and she intended to report what she had seen when she got back into the office. Maybe they could use some of their narcotics officers and organise a raid.

For now, though, there was nothing she could do without causing an unholy ruckus and getting Hal and his band fired for being friends of the Plod as well as the evidence probably being spirited away and making her feel a fool. She decided to leave it to the people who knew how to handle these things.

In the meantime, her son was improving, with the possibility that he might be able to come home in a day or two, and her level of anxiety had decreased considerably. Granted, there were still two cases of murder most ghastly to solve, and a missing girl to find, but then what was life in Littleton-on-Sea if not full of the low and downright unpleasant?

All in all, they had a good night, with some really great music from the band. They had improved beyond recognition since she had last attended one of Hal's gigs, and that must be why the group was so much in demand now. Making a conscious effort, she kept her mind empty of everything except enjoying herself. Towards the end of the evening however she noticed that Lauren was not drinking, and leaned over to shout into her ear to enquire why.

'I think I'd better get home tonight. I could do with doing some laundry, and if I get back late, I might be able to get it on without the pathetic performance from beyond the annexe door. I *am* having a good time, but I have to exercise some sort of responsibility. I can't just abandon the place and stop keeping myself clean and tidy.' When was the woman anything other than pristine? thought Olivia, but she let it go. Lauren was old enough to make her own decisions.

'You know you'd have been welcome to stay with us and do your smalls in our machine,' she replied.

'That's very kind of you, but I just want to keep an eye on the place. They'll be gone soon, and I want to make sure that that bitch doesn't go off with anything of mine, at least anything that I value. I wouldn't put anything past her. She's already stolen my husband from beneath my nose, and I don't want her doing the same with my jewellery. I shall take that into the bank tomorrow, ask them to put it in a safety deposit box for a while until I stop feeling vulnerable on my own.'

'Do you want Leon to drop you off home?'

'No, my car's at yours, and I've had nothing since I left your place hours ago, and then it was only one small – well, small-ish – glass of wine.'

They didn't get back to the cottage until a little after

midnight, but it was a merry group that rolled out of Leon's van. Olivia even went so far as to hug Lauren goodnight, a gesture that was definitely not in her normal repertoire. Leon chugged away in his old bus with a wave out of the driver's window, and Hal opened the cottage door. The two women waved goodbye, and Lauren went over to her car, rummaging through her handbag to locate her keys.

As she strapped herself in, she suddenly felt apprehensive. It was all very well declaring that she had to act responsibly when she was sitting in a dimly lit club with a friend. It was quite another to think of running into Kenneth or Gerda even at this late hour, and she sent up a little prayer that they would be long asleep when she slipped into the house.

As she drew up at the old barn a hideous thought lodged in her head. The man wouldn't have had the audacity to change the locks, would he, or the code on the alarm system? Her key inserted in the door she twisted it and, with a great sigh of relief, she felt the lock give. It had been a mad few seconds thinking about the other possibilities, and she realised that, if Kenneth earned just a bit less, and didn't have such good prospects, it was something that might well have happened.

As quietly as she could she slipped off her coat and shoes and put them away in the hall cupboard. Leaving her handbag by the stairs, she made her way to the kitchen. No lights were burning, but she still felt her hands trembling and damp with sweat. She couldn't wait until the day arrived when they would both go, and she could just look forward to seeing the children again. She really would have to speak to that local school about them attending.

Perhaps they could start after Christmas, she thought as she switched on the light. With a flash of panic, she realised she could hear the sound of someone else breathing, and turned round to face the bogey. She had almost no time at all to realise that Kenneth was standing right behind her, before his fist hit the bridge of her glasses. They broke into two halves, and she could see the blurry impression of drops of blood falling to the ground.

Why the hell had he done that? She'd done nothing wrong. It was he who had committed adultery. She was paralysed with shock, and could neither move to pick up her broken glasses, nor move away to get something to stem the bleeding from her nose. 'What was that for?' she asked in a tremulous voice with little volume.

'Why couldn't you just stay at home and be the wife I wanted, instead of having to go running back to work as soon as the children were approaching school age. You've brought all this on yourself.'

'How?'

'If you'd just stayed here and managed without a nanny for your precious working shifts, I'd never have thought of another woman, but you got so wrapped up in your precious *job* that I felt alienated in my own home – and God knows I pay enough for it.'

'And what was I supposed to do when you were away working?' asked Lauren, still stunned by his accusation.

'You could have taken on some good works, so that you were free for me when I was here. As it is, you were so taken up with your working life that our relationship just withered and died.'

'You mean you wanted me to be a virtual prisoner, on call for if and when you needed my services?'

'No. I wanted you to be here with me for all the hours I was at home.'

'You could have taken us all with you. There are English schools out there, or they could have boarded and flown out to us in the school holidays.'

'When I suggested it once, you said you didn't want to, and you were so vehement about not wanting to live in that particular country that I never brought it up again.'

'I might not have been keen, but how could I know that my marriage depended on it?'

'You couldn't, and neither could I. This time you've reaped what you have sown. This is all your doing, and I wanted you to be aware of that.'

Lauren didn't know how she did it, but she pulled back a fist and thumped Kenneth right in the eye, making him stagger and put his hand up to the injured area. 'If you touch me again I shall press charges for assault,' she informed him, a ring of steel in her voice. How dare he blame his own infidelity on her!

'I want you out of my kitchen now, or I'm going to call the police. I need to do some laundry, I want to do it in peace, and I don't want to set eyes on you or your tart before you leave. Just get out of my house and leave me alone.'

He turned on his heel and left her. As she loaded dirty laundry into the machine and set it going, she decided she'd have to get a bolt for that door. She'd do it first thing in the morning. If he ever came back to stay there to visit the children – if there was nothing she could legally do to stop him – at least she could stop him entering the house at his leisure. She'd also have to be the one that had all the locks changed and change the code on the burglar alarm. She couldn't risk him just waltzing into the house whenever he wanted something.

In her bedroom, she pushed Kenneth's erstwhile bedside table against the door, stripped off her clothes, and got into bed. She simply was too stunned to be bothered with a shower. Her nose hurt abominably, and she'd taken some time to clean up the blood and find her spare set of glasses, but it was with a sense of history repeating itself she cried herself to sleep again.

The following morning, one look in the bathroom mirror told her that she wouldn't be able to hide what had happened; she had no chance of keeping Kenneth's inexplicable violence to herself. Both her eyes were blackening, and her nose was red and swollen. The bruising had drained down to below her eyes, so that even sunglasses wouldn't hide her shameful state, nor avoid enquiries as to how it had happened.

She could, of course, lie, but that would do her no good whatsoever. If she told people she'd had an accident, they might think her clumsy or even a drunk. No, she'd have to let everyone know that her high-flyer husband, as well as being unfaithful to her with the au pair, had also punched her on the nose for daring to have a life outside the house. She had no intention of covering up for his unreasonable behaviour, and if he told anyone that she'd thumped him, then perhaps she might get the chance to tell whomever he'd told exactly *why* she'd hit him. He'd started it.

Now she began to feel childish, but then things like this probably made everyone feel a bit infantile. Maybe Kenneth would claim that he'd hit her back, that she'd hit him first. Oh, what the hell. She'd just tell the whole story, including the bit where she'd struck him. Her reaction didn't seem unreasonable, given the circumstances.

Dammit, she'd leave buying the bolt for the annexe door until her way home. Kenneth wouldn't dare have the locks changed, denying his children shelter when they would be home in only a few weeks, and he simply didn't have enough time to legally get possession of it. He'd be gone very soon, and she'd just have to brazen things out. All that time spent on her own during term-time – Gerda hardly counted as company – had made her a stronger person, and she still had the diversion of her work to keep her mind occupied.

When she got into the office she found Olivia already there, looking grey with exhaustion, her clothes the same ones as she had been wearing the night before and her desk covered with paperwork.

'What happened to you?' she asked, getting the question in first before her boss asked it. 'How long have you been here?'

'Since about one a.m.,' came the bleak reply.

'But you were sozzled when I left just after midnight,' replied Lauren with surprise.

'It's amazing how sobering another dead body can be, when coupled with several cups of very strong coffee and a taxi to stop one losing one's licence,' she replied, somewhat grandly.

'Whose body?' asked Lauren, with a sinking feeling in her stomach, Kenneth now completely forgotten.

'Genni Lacey's.'

'Oh, no. Where was she found? Who found her? Any idea what happened to her? Was it an accident that went unreported?'

'Whoa, Sergeant. Let me start at the beginning. She was found bundled into one of the commercial wheelie bins at the back of the River View pub by the landlord, when he took out the rubbish after he'd closed up and cleared away. Her body had clearly been dumped; no sign of an accident. We have no evidence yet of who did it, but I still reckon on our quartet of usual suspects, and I'm going to have to step up our investigations now there has been a third murder.

'It looks like she died from an injected overdose of drugs, but not straight after she disappeared. This was no unreported accident: this was cold-blooded murder, and it also looks as if she'd been raped violently several times. I'm waiting on results from Dylan MacArthur. We got him out of bed and he said he'd start on it straightaway. There's madness here, or just pure, unadulterated evil.'

'Was she beaten like the others?' asked Lauren, a moue of disgust wrinkling her nose painfully.

'She'd been slapped around a little, but the most prominent marks were bite marks. We've got some sick pervert, or perverts, plural, on our hands.'

'Have her parents been informed?'

It was only this far into their conversation that Olivia looked up enough to notice that Lauren had received some sort of trauma to her face, and her mouth fell open in disbelief. Without hesitation, she asked, 'Did Kenneth do that to you? Or Gerda? Why?'

'Kenneth. Because I've got a life,' she replied, and then burst into laughter that soon became hysterical, and Olivia had to give her a slap across the cheek to stop her.

'Thanks a bunch, guv. I actually needed that.' Before she could continue, the DI's phone rang and she answered it almost as a reflex reaction. After a couple of minutes, mainly of listening, she put down the handset and turned to Lauren.

'Sorry to rain on your parade, but our guy from that nasty head-on has come round – remember the man so full of drugs that he went straight into another car and killed three people? He's talking about drugs, and it sounds as if he wants to get something off his chest, in return for immunity. Well, we'll see about that. We'll let him unburden himself, first, shall we? The only promises on offer are of the pie-crust variety at the moment. Come on, Raccoon-Face, we've got a job to do.' Raccoon-Face was a risk, but Lauren didn't seem to take it amiss.

'Please don't make me laugh, boss. It hurts. And why are you treating this as a priority?'

'Because I think that everything's part and parcel of the same thing: the supposed abduction, the two first murders, the drugs in this town, and this guy that was so pumped full of drugs that he fell unconscious at the wheel of his car. Maybe even this latest body.'

'How can you be sure? Is there any evidence?'

'None whatsoever,' replied Olivia, 'but as sure as I'm riding this unicycle, they're part and parcel of the same thing.' Pause. 'Don't laugh. It'll hurt.'

'It does.'

They were allowed only just over ten minutes with the man from the accident, whose name turned out to be Peter Hanger; Cliff to his friends and associates. He kept lapsing back into a state of either unconsciousness or sleep while they questioned him, but they did glean enough information to know that he was bringing a big cache of illegal drugs down to the town. There was to be a big drive to up sales and sort out those dealers who were ripping off the management.

He told them he had been asked to get together with some of the local members of the gang and sort out a list of names that only *he* had, but which he had not read at the time. He had been more nervous of what was expected of him, for he was not usually a violent man. The car had been stuffed with drugs, and as he had become a user, he couldn't resist testing the merchandise. Unfortunately for him it had proved purer than he was used to, hence the car crash.

He'd never met the boss of the ring and had always received his instructions from someone on an unidentifiable phone with a heavily disguised voice. It had seemed the sort of stuff that cheap movies were made of, but he'd never questioned it because he had some serious gambling debts, and the work paid well.

'Can't you remember the names on the list, or how many of them there were?' asked Hardy. 'I'm sure you couldn't have resisted the temptation to have a quick butcher's.'

He had replied that he had had just a quick squint at them – he thought – but things had become blurry since his accident, and he couldn't remember anything in any detail until some hours before the accident happened.

At that point they were ejected from his room as he needed to rest. Hardy observed that it was just as well that the man had been involved in an accident, or he might be involved in a murder case by now, but she wished she had been able to prise his local contact out of him, and who was on that hit list.

'I'd bet my shirt on it being our first two murder victims, and somehow I've got to tie up that abduction and murder with it too. I know it seems unlikely, but I can feel it in my water that they're connected.'

'It could have been a list of local goons,' suggested Lauren. 'Why don't we get those men in again and re-question them? We can leave the driver to the Drugs Squad.'

'Good idea.'

As they went to leave the ward they were approached by a nurse.

'Yes, Sister,' said Hardy, 'what can we do for you?'

'Are you the two detectives that came in to question our unconscious man?'

'We are, indeed.'

'I thought so,' said the nurse, 'only, I've just heard from one of my colleagues that that little girl that was so seriously injured in the other car involved in the accident …'

'Yes, go on,' Hardy prompted her.

'They've done tests for brain death. I know it seems a bit early, but there really seemed so little hope for her, and the results have just come through. I'm afraid she is brain-dead, and her father is being asked to come in to discuss when – and if, I suppose – we turn off her life support machine. Poor man, to lose his wife and his daughter so tragically.'

'That'll be another charge of causing death by dangerous driving,' commented DI Hardy in her official voice, her face as hard as marble.

Back in the car, Hardy dissolved noisily into tears and, when her sergeant asked her what was the matter, she replied, 'It was only a few days ago that my own son was in there, and we didn't know whether he was going to live or die. I've been so lucky, and I should stop feeling sorry for myself.'

'Nonsense. You've been through a dreadful time.'

'So have you,' retorted the DI, trying her hardest to pull herself together. 'Now, describe to me how you got those two lovely black eyes,' and she sang the last four words, making Groves simultaneously smile and wince with pain. 'Come on, let's stop off at mine for a very quick coffee so you can tell me in complete privacy.'

CHAPTER NINE

As Olivia was spluttering with rage at what Kenneth had done and said, simultaneously making coffee – the good stuff this time – Lauren noticed that her boss walked with a slight limp that she had never observed before.

'You didn't fall over last night when we got back, did you?' she asked.

'Whatever makes you think that?' Olivia was obviously surprised at the question.

'Because you were rather pissed last night, pardon my language, and today you seem to be limping a bit. I just wondered if, in the hurry to sober up and get back to the station, you might have twisted your ankle.'

'If only it were that simple,' she replied. 'It only happens when I'm very tired, and after the last few days that I've had, followed by a night on the lash and then being called back into work to deal with another grisly murder, you can imagine that I'm not as fresh as a daisy.'

'Go on, then,' Lauren urged her.

'I got shot. Simple as that.'

'You were shot?' Lauren's eyebrows nearly disappeared into her hairline, causing her considerable facial pain. 'So what happened?'

'I'm surprised some of the older staff haven't told you. It was back when I was a PC, and the drugs squad was looking for volunteers for a raid on a notorious club on the seafront – it's not there now. It burnt down a few years ago. Anyway, PC Muggins here volunteers, we went in mob-handed – stupid really – and some guy pulls out a gun, which we didn't expect – we had no idea there were any firearms, not like nowadays when we know there usually will be. The guy with the gun shouts a warning and then I get this burning feeling in my calf.

'He said he was aiming for the floor just as a warning, but does my leg look like flooring? It's not as if I was sylph-like and he'd hardly noticed my slender existence. I was the same tub I am now. Anyway, that scared the life out of his mates – and him, incidentally, and he threw the gun to the floor. We got our arrests, and I got rather a lot of sick leave and a bowl of fruit – and, of course, this slight limp when I'm knackered.'

'That must have been awful.'

'Not as awful as having my husband punch me on the nose because my job was the reason for his infidelity, as if you ought to apologise to him for what you put him through in just having a life. God, if I ever meet this husband of yours, I think I'll floor him.'

'You won't get a chance. I think they're going tonight, to spend a night in the airport hotel, and they can't get out of my house soon enough for my liking.'

'You're very brave. I couldn't bear it if that happened between me and Hal.'

'It's not bravery, it's the realisation that our marriage has been fatally flawed for years now, and that, although his salary's been useful, I'd rather not have him attached to it. It's been a sham for so long, I can't even remember when I got tired of being used like a sex toy every night without complaint.'

'Every night?'

'That's right.'

'I'm surprised you haven't castrated him.'

'I have thought of it. I'm probably the only woman in the world who looks forward to her periods, just to be left in peace for a while.'

'Jesus!'

PCs Franklin and Shuttleworth were dispatched to

round up Messrs. Edwards, Stoner, Lord and Trussler, while Hardy and Groves went to the Laceys' house to question the parents further. Although the parents had provided the police with her last school photograph, DI Hardy didn't think this was really representative of how she may have looked on the last night of her life, particularly bearing in mind what had been found in her bedroom.

The two officers came armed with some photographs that had been printed from those on the girl's computer, most of them selfies or shots with groups of friends, and they needed her parents to identify the friends that she usually hung about with, and who might have either been with her or egged her on to something she might not normally do.

It was not something that either of them looked forward to, but they were grateful to the young PC, Teri Friend, who had proved to have a real gift for breaking bad news and comforting those who were bereaved. At least they hadn't had to do that.

When they arrived, the door was answered by PC Friend herself, who had stayed on to keep the Laceys company in the first hours of their loss. She knew she was a sounding board, and was excellent at dealing with anything that was thrown at her – they could either talk about their lost loved one, or rant on about the unfairness of it all.

'Come in,' she invited them in a hushed tone, calling into the living room, 'DI Hardy and DS Groves are here to speak to you, Mr and Mrs Lacey.' Both parents were huddled together on the sofa, their arms round each other, tears still running down their faces, but they were silent in their extremity of shock and grief, and didn't even look up when the two new arrivals entered the room.

'Sir, madam, we'd like to ask you a few questions about your daughter's friends and the day she disappeared,' DI Hardy began.

'We've told you everything we know. We haven't got anything else to say,' replied the father, looking up from his wife's shoulder.

'We've brought some photographs printed from your daughter's computer, pictures of Genni with some of her friends, and we wondered if you could identify them for us, so that we might start questioning them to see if anyone was with her the day she disappeared, or if someone egged her on – maybe dared her – to do something risky and out of character. I wonder if you'd be good enough to take some time to look at them?'

The DI handed a group of photos to Mrs Lacey, and perched on the edge of a chair, Groves following suit so that she didn't stand out. As the bereaved mother began to sob, the sergeant got out her notebook and Hardy put a small tape recorder on the coffee table with a mumbled, 'I hope you don't mind.'

As Mrs Lacey began to cry as if her heart would break, her husband said, 'I think we can tell you who most of these girls are, but our Genni's almost unrecognisable under all that make-up.'

'We did wonder about that. She doesn't look at all like she looked in that school photo, does she? Perhaps you would be kind enough to give us permission to use one of those we have printed, to put it out with another appeal for any information about sightings.'

Lauren noted down three names as being those of her current best friends. 'But you know what teenage girls are like – this week's enemy is last week's best friend,' added Abi shakily through her tears. 'There are some others here, but she'd either fallen out with them recently, or wasn't particularly friendly with them anymore. They're just on the periphery of her group now.'

'You said she was wearing a T-shirt and jeans when she went out?'

'Yes, but she had her rucksack with her. After seeing what was in her bedroom, she could have had anything in there ... but surely you know what she was wearing, if you've found her ... her body.'

'I'm afraid not, Mrs Lacey.'

'My God, you're not saying she was naked when she was found, are you? And had she been interfered with?'

PC Friend went over to the couple and took the spare space on the sofa so that she could comfort Mrs Lacey, who had once again disintegrated into heartbroken sobs. 'My poor little baby. My poor little girl.'

'Thank you for these names. We'll go to their homes and question them, and we'll let you know if we find out anything else. Thank you very much for your co-operation in your time of loss.' Olivia hated the platitudes that had attached themselves to loss and death, but knew that they had to be observed and paid lip service to, or she might be accused of being flint-hearted and uncaring.

Franklin and Shuttleworth had had a bit of a game laying hands on the men who were wanted for questioning, but eventually they'd run them all to ground, Shuttleworth's impressive build making sure that none of them tried to resist arrest. When they got their quarries back to the station, however, each of the men had insisted on having his solicitor present before they answered any questions. Having got their solicitors, however, they then said nothing more. This was still the situation when the DI and DS arrived there: the men sitting silently, with their cups of hot, stickily sweet tea, which they had been provided with courtesy of the duty officer.

Olivia and Lauren brought the broad figure of Shuttleworth to stand in the room with them while they taped the interviews, once the 'briefs' had arrived, and they questioned the men for the rest of the afternoon about what they had been doing on the evening in question, when Genni had disappeared, but to no avail.

They all told the same story: that they had been hanging around the town, popped into a couple of pubs for a drink, and then shared a takeaway. For some reason, the last bit of this group alibi seemed to amuse each one of them, but Hardy allowed that to lie for now.

Lauren had finally got the house to herself, and Ben Hardy had been allowed home from hospital to his parents' home. Enquiries were ongoing in all three murders, as well as into the source of the drugs that had been found in Peter Hanger's car, but Hanger himself had lapsed into a coma again, this time not an induced one, and they would have to bide their time.

There was a grim atmosphere in the station, with the unsolved crimes still hanging around, and even the town had taken on an air of wariness and fear, the streets being even more empty in the evenings than would usually have been expected of November. Pubs and clubs were under-attended, and parents kept a much closer eye on their teenage children for fear that whoever was out there hadn't finished his grisly business yet.

It was into this atmosphere of apprehension and barely supressed horror that the news of another body arrived at the station. A local man who kept a fishing boat for pleasure had decided to take a trip to see if he could catch anything on a line. His boat had been stored inside a large unused boat shed, once part of the bustling local fishing community but now deserted and rotting. Once he'd got the boat into the main water he'd reached for the line from his metal mooring ring, and found a great resistance on the end of it. Someone had clearly tied something to the ring.

Instead of wasting time wondering what on earth could be tied to his ring, he yanked on it hard, eventually drawing forth a sack with what looked like the remains of a human head sticking out of it; one not very fresh and terribly nibbled and chewed. After throwing up his breakfast into the river, he immediately called 999 on his mobile and asked for the police.

There was a car at the scene inside ten minutes, and the sometime fisherman was told that a medic was on the way, along with a CSI team and CID. As they waited for reinforcements to arrive, the man, James Lister, now with a cool head since the contents of his stomach were dispensed with, said, 'He's gonna be a bugger to identify in that state, isn't he? Have you not had anybody reported missing?'

The uniformed officers shrugged off the question and waited for their superiors to arrive. Their lot was just to keep schtum and monitor the situation, making sure that the scene wasn't tampered with.

The pile of sodden remains on the ground was the only ugly thing in sight. It was a beautifully bright November morning, with a clear blue sky, the sun twinkling on the little wavelets of the river. The surrounding fields were covered with frost, making them shine like fields of jewels, and cobwebs appeared as delicate works of the finest filigree.

Into this almost perfect autumnal scene marched DI Hardy and DS Groves, originally rejoicing in the perfect day, but feeling the waves of trepidation wash over them as they approached the group of men on the bank. What had turned up now? They had been told there was a body in some sort of bag, but there had been no other concrete information. They had just been given the location and told to go out there.

Superintendent Devenish was beginning to lose his rag at the lack of progress on the investigations, and was worried about pressure from above, or – even worse – having officers brought in over the heads of his team, relieving him of the responsibility for clearing up the crimes and locking away the villains. Devenish, like

Sherlock Holmes before him, had no taste for the modern equivalent of being taken over by Scotland Yard.

It was that same night that Lauren began to get silent phone calls in the early hours, all of which had the number withheld. At first she just thought it was a wrong number, but when her sleep had been disturbed five times, she began to get worried.

Did someone know she was newly on her own, and was trying to rattle her? Or was it someone connected with the case threatening her with their silence? When she confided in Olivia the next day, the senior officer largely shrugged it off, telling her to either change her number or get the phone company to monitor her calls. She told her sergeant that she could even make an official complaint here in the station, but Lauren didn't want to make any more fuss than was necessary.

INTERLUDE

In his office in the club he owned near the sea, the man put down the telephone. He would have to step up the pressure if he was going to get everyone in line. His current tactics weren't working at all. Maybe he'd have to call on his team again, but he'd need to rap some knuckles at the same time. Actions like that last one had not been requested and it was totally unacceptable. If he didn't get them back under his thumb before long, he'd lose his grip, and his London contact.

That should be sorted out, now. The phone call should deal with any loose cannons very effectively.

CHAPTER TEN

DI Hardy called her team together to sum up what they had so far although, if she were honest with herself, she was currently motivated more by a gut feeling than overwhelming physical evidence.

'We have four strong suspects for all this mayhem in our town; everyone else who was interviewed has had independent corroboration of their whereabouts at the times of the crimes. These four provide mutual alibis for each other and it stinks. All we have to do now is prove it,' she stated. 'We're waiting for Forensics, and I've had some of you collecting the available CCTV footage. There's also a request for a television appeal to anyone who might have been in a pub or takeaway that evening, and who could place those four anywhere at a particular time, so we need to put their photographs out for that. A new photo of Genni Lacey has been issued, this time in trendy clothes and with lashings of make-up. The girl's three friends have not been forthcoming with any information, so we are relying on members of the public with a good memory to help us out.

'Colin, all I need now is for you to go through the CCTV stuff and see if there's anything that might back up what we think we know so far.'

Colin Redwood gave a deep sigh as the menial task was thrust upon him. He thought he was worth much more than that, and should be in the thick of things, wherever the thick happened to be.

'It's a very important job, Colin,' said Hardy. 'Don't put it down. You could discover the vital piece of visual evidence.' This did little to reassure him that he was a valued member of the team, but it did reinforce that he was also one of the most junior. He was, all things considered, totally pissed off. This wasn't how he had envisaged life in the police at all. He silently vowed to sort Hardy out.

'We're waiting on some DNA evidence from the post-mortem, which could be an important breakthrough for us, and we'll take it from there. The new body from the river will have to be identified, and I just hope that someone who could get themselves killed like that won't turn out to be a model citizen, but will be identifiable from our national database. We'll carry on with our routine enquiries until we get something solid on those two matters. Colin, I've set aside a little room for you to go through all the CCTV footage, so off you all go. We've got plenty to do, with lots of supposed sightings of the girl who went missing as well. Get to it. In the meantime, I've got a CSI team going through that boatshed with a fine tooth comb.'

The rest of the day followed a well-established routine, without any startling developments, but full of the things that had to be done – even if only to say that they had been. There was no one of any seniority who would back a hunch and let them cut corners.

'I'm still fairly sure we've got our men,' Hardy confided to Lauren before they finished for the day. 'Let's hope we've got two matches from the database by tomorrow morning, so that we can push forward with our enquiries, and home in on those four slimy sods. They need locking up and the key throwing away.'

When Lauren got home, the whole house, including the annexe, was in darkness, much to her consternation. When she unlocked the door, she flipped on a light and checked that the alarm was on, just to make sure that there were no unwelcome visitors waiting for her inside. That proven, however, she still went through every room just to make sure, checking that all the windows and exterior doors were closed and locked.

When she got into the kitchen, she found a note from Kenneth on the kitchen table, informing her that he and Gerda had left earlier that day, because they couldn't stand being locked into the tiny annexe while she swanned around in the whole house. Lauren was infuriated. For a start, they hadn't been *locked in*, but were free to go where they pleased, certainly when she was at work. It wasn't as if she had security cameras in place. For another, it was completely their fault that things had worked out how they did. It had nothing to do with her that Kenneth couldn't keep it in his trousers. She hadn't asked for the marriage to end this way, although she had to admit that it would had to have come to an end sooner or later.

Taking a quick peek, she noticed that the lovers had left their living quarters in complete disarray, and she slammed shut the door with a deep sigh of martyrdom. That was one way of getting back at her: to cause her inconvenience and unwelcome work, while driving home just who had caused that mess. It was petty but, in hindsight, it was typical of Kenneth.

That evening she drank a couple of glasses of wine to relax her and went to bed with her thoughts on the children. She'd have to contact the local school soon, to get them on the roll before Christmas, which wasn't very far away, and tell their boarding schools that they would be leaving at the end of term.

Thinking of Christmas crystallised her thoughts. Surely the current case would be closed by then and, if it was, she had a good mind to take some leave and take the children to her parents' house. She didn't think she could face the festive season with Kenneth and Gerda once again in the annexe, and the bewilderment and upset that this would cause the kids.

They were quite used to Kenneth being away and for a

while, at least, she wouldn't have to say anything about him leaving the family unit. They would just take it as normal that he wasn't around and, even if they did question the fact that he wasn't home for Christmas, she could explain that he wasn't in a Christian country and, therefore, Christmas wasn't a holiday over there. The added bonus of seeing their grandparents should bridge the gap that his absence left. If Kenneth wanted to see the children it would be on her terms.

As she dropped off to sleep, the phone rang and woke her. It was another silent call, but she could hear breathing in the background. Instead of frightening her, it made her mad. How could anyone want to terrorise her? If it was anything to do with work, surely she wasn't of sufficient rank to be the victim of such a campaign of silence? Surely it couldn't be Kenneth's idea of a joke?

She eventually went back to sleep, only to be woken at 3.20 by the urgent beeping of the smoke alarm. As she came back to consciousness, she smelled smoke with a suspicious hint of petrol behind it, and shot out of bed, running to the top of the stairs to check on the situation.

On the hall floor, a patch of flame was just catching hold. Rushing for a blanket from the airing cupboard, she threw it down the stairs with an immaculate aim, then followed it down, grabbing a fire extinguisher from the landing, one of two that the insurance company had insisted they install due to the remote situation of the property.

She grabbed the phone from the hall table, frantically tramping on the blanket, dialled 999 and put the phone on to speaker. She then let loose with the fire extinguisher, shouting to be heard from her position just by the front door, hoping to God that this was the only seat of the fire. If they'd set fires at other points around the house, she was toast.

Having requested the fire service and checked that the

fire was all but out, she continued with the contents of the fire extinguisher, leaving the scene for a moment to fetch the one from the kitchen, along with a fire blanket from beside the cooker, only noticing when the danger was all but passed, that her feet were somewhat burnt and very tender.

A police car arrived on the heels of the fire service, and when the fire service had done everything they could, a man was left on guard, as the house could no longer be secured, and she asked to be taken to Olivia's house. There was nowhere else she could think of going, and she didn't want to lie in the dark knowing that the phone was sure to ring again any minute.

She could ring the insurance company in the morning and arrange for the work to be done and the house made secure. Making a note to check that Kenneth hadn't blocked her access to the bank account, she suddenly realised she was shaking. What was happening to her well-ordered life? It seemed to have descended into chaos.

Olivia was very surprised to be awoken at such an hour, but readily accepted Lauren into the house, gave her yet another sleeping tablet, and immediately installed her in Hibbie's still-vacant room. There was enough time in the morning to deal with whatever had happened, and neither of them would be served by losing the rest of the night's sleep. She'd lost enough sleep over Ben's crisis, without compounding her tiredness.

When the inspector got back to bed, her thoughts had firmly homed in on Ben. He had denied taking any drugs, but had insisted that he'd been given spiked drinks. She couldn't really believe this, and was sure that he was so ashamed of what had happened that he just couldn't take responsibility for it. Although his one-time friend had been banned from the house, she didn't see him as a kid who would deliberately put drugs into his friend's drink.

She thought it more than likely that Ben had taken them by choice, and then been terrified by the outcome and not been able to own up to his foolish actions. She'd have to get Hibbie to have a talk with him when she got home, Hibbie had always been able to influence Ben, and Olivia always thought that she seemed more mature despite being younger And where exactly was she? Surely it wasn't anywhere near half term now? She had always allowed Hibbie more freedom because of her maturity, didn't feel the need to check up on her all the time, and now it seemed as if her daughter didn't want to confide in her at all.

She seemed to have taken a wrong turning with her kids, both of them. And she wasn't sure where she'd gone wrong, but what with Ben's overdose and Hibbie not wanting to be at home any more than she had to, something was wrong. Would it eventually cost her her job, or her relationship with her children?

She'd only spoken to her daughter a couple of times on her mobile since she'd been gone and she couldn't' remember exactly when Hibbie had embarked on this lengthy stay with a friend. What had happened to her relationship with her daughter that they'd drifted so far apart? She'd have to give her a ring tomorrow and see what was going on. What with all the uncharacteristically grisly murders in the town, she, too, was beginning to think that her life was spiralling out of control.

Breakfast proved to be a defining get-together, as Lauren disclosed details of exactly what had happened since she had got home the night before. Olivia told her that she had to stay with her for a while as it obviously wasn't safe for her to go back to her own place. 'You have to keep your distance until we determine whether this is just a scare campaign by Kenneth to punish you, or whether it has something to do with the current cases. You won't be safe until we've got these murders wrapped up, and I can't take the responsibility of letting you go back,' she informed her sergeant forcefully.

'I know, I know it's nothing to do with you, but you have to wonder how his mind works. He's already blamed you for being a bad wife. Is it beyond the realms of possibility that he might want to scare the wits out of you as his revenge?'

'That's all very well, but what if your daughter comes back soon?' countered Lauren.

'There's always the spare room. Let's just wait until your house is secure again, and then we can consider you going back, but with the house under surveillance, in case whoever it is has another go.'

'You know there aren't the resources to cover that.'

'We'll sort something out. And I must get in touch with Hibbie today. She's been gone rather a long time and, what with Ben and everything else that's going on, I've completely lost track of how long she's been gone. I don't know what's come over her, she's usually so reliable.'

'And I've got schools and my parents to phone, not to mention the insurance company.'

'Come on, we'll go over to yours to collect whatever you need and your car, then we'll take things from there. Oh, and collect your flute as well. If you're staying here, there's no reason why we shouldn't have some fun at the same time.'

CHAPTER ELEVEN

The office was buzzing when they got in. The DNA results were through from Genni Lacey's post-mortem, and the sample had been matched to Dennis Trussler. When they got in, one of the DCs shouted the name at Hardy, attracting her attention, but Lauren was more surprised to see the expression on Colin Redwood's face. It had an expression of astonishment on it that she could not explain.

'Right, troops,' Hardy called. 'We need Trussler in again for questioning. No doubt he'll still have his brief hanging on to his shirt-tails, but we've got a forensic link to that poor girl now, and I think we have to drive it home. He's definitely in the frame. All four of them are in this together, I know they are. All we have to do to Trussler is crack him, and point out to him that he doesn't have to take all the blame.'

Teri Friend was dispatched along with the burly frame of Liam Shuttleworth to do the deed, and the whole office held its breath. If they could wrap it up, there would be kudos all round.

In the interim, Hardy decided to bring Lauren up to speed on Trussler, one of their regular customers. 'He was always going to come to a bad end. He's been in and out of prison and trouble with the police, as I told you before. As far as I know, he's living with a woman called Mary Mackintosh and her two kids on the big council estate that sprawls over to the river.

'He's got a record of petty crime that would be quite impressive for a man twenty years older, and yet he's so often got off with a clever brief or lack of corroborating evidence. He's as slippery as an eel, and I'd really love to nail him once and for all. He's pretty unpleasant, which I'm sure you'd agree from what you've seen already, and I'd throw a party if he was finally put away for a long time.'

'What about the other three?' asked Lauren.

'We'll leave them to stew. Trussler's the obvious ringleader, and now we've got something definite on him. Very careless not to check that your rubber's in one piece.'

'Do you think he'll talk?'

'Eventually, if he thinks he's going to get a deal out of it. He's nobody's fool, except, obviously, when it comes to his dick.'

But they were going to have to wait a while before they enjoyed Mr Trussler's company. He had proved elusive when Friend and Shuttleworth had called at his house. Mary Mackintosh had even invited them in to take a look round the house to see if they could find him. She said she had no idea where he was, but that she'd do for him when he got back. He'd left her without a penny in her purse, and she'd run out of fags.

'The poor woman was just rummaging down the back of the settee when we arrived. I wish her luck with that. It was pretty grubby, and if she's got kids, there could be anything down there,' added Teri Friend. 'Although it looked like he'd said goodbye with his fists. She had a bruised cheek and a split lip.'

'What about that bloke found in the river?' asked the sergeant, suddenly remembering the new victim with stomach-churning vividness, and blushing at the thought of her own bruising underneath the thick foundation she had adopted since Kenneth had landed her one. That sort of behaviour had nothing to do with class, and everything to do with an explosive nature.

'Should be a report in later today.' Hardy said, 'I just hope he's on the database. The chances are that he is, if he's been wiped out by this lot. And it shouldn't be too long before we get some forensic evidence back from that boatshed.'

Hardy and Groves went round to Trussler's house, to see if they could either locate him or encourage any information out of his girlfriend. When the battered woman opened the door, letting the sounds of a couple of kids shouting against the noise of the television escape, Lauren had her second shock of the working day. She knew that face beneath the bruises; she just couldn't work out where from.

They learnt nothing they didn't already know, except for the fact that he'd said he'd got a 'meet' and wouldn't be back till late the night before. 'Never mind,' said Hardy, as they left. 'We'll give him another tug ourselves later on. If nothing else, we can spur that girlfriend of his to get in touch with him to tell him that higher ranks are after him now.'

The afternoon was to prove busier than expected. Just after lunch Hardy and Groves left the station and headed for Trussler's address to see if they could actually run the man to ground. Mary Mackintosh answered the door, and caused Lauren to stare at her face again, as she had done to a few other people lately.

'May we have a word with Mr Trussler, please?' asked Hardy.

Putting her hand to her split lip, Ms Mackintosh replied, 'I haven't seen him since yesterday, I told you earlier on. Nothing's changed since then. If he's gone after a bird, I'll skin him alive. Me and my kids haven't got anywhere else to go, so he needn't think he can just throw us out and move in a new model.'

This sounded very much like the truth, and they would have to leave this until tomorrow now. They'd badgered the injured woman enough for one day. As they drove back to the station, however, Lauren said, 'I'm sure I know that woman from somewhere. I know she's got that facial bruising but even so, I'm sure I've seen her somewhere before.'

'Any idea where?' Hardy was anxious to get things sorted out.

'Not at the moment. It may have been at my last station. I'll have to put it on "search and retrieve".'

'What the hell's that when it's at home?' asked Hardy.

Lauren began to bluster with embarrassment. 'It's just something I do with my brain. Promise you won't make fun of me?'

Hardy promised, but with her fingers crossed out of sight.

'If I concentrate very deeply and mutter the words "search and retrieve", it seems like a little man in a brown coat goes off down the corridors of my memory, going through all the filing cabinets. Usually within a few hours, the answer comes to me. I can't explain it – it's just what happens.'

Thinking *bonkers*, Olivia nevertheless said, 'If it works for you, don't knock it.'

Later that afternoon, the latest edition of the local paper came out, and one was delivered to the inspector as soon as it had hit the streets. There must have been a 'hold the front page' moment, because the headline was *Local Man Named in Multiple Murder Enquiry*. Trussler was named in the accompanying article, and Hardy almost burst her boiler cursing and swearing.

'How the bloody hell did they get Trussler's name? It hasn't been uttered outside this office, not to my knowledge. And how did they get all this other stuff, like it looks like he's gone underground?'

'It must have been his girlfriend,' suggested Lauren.

'My arse, it was the girlfriend. I could understand her

going to a tabloid to get some extra fag money, but this local outfit can't afford to pay for information. Anyway, we never told her why we wanted to talk to him. No, we've got a leak amongst our ranks: that's the only explanation. There's a mole here, and I intend to find out who it is.'

As she finished this dramatic statement the whole office fell silent. 'Who's missing?'

The answer turned out to be, only Colin Redwood, who was said to have been shut in the little office looking at CCTV footage since just after the start of the working day.

'Check on that, will you?' Hardy called to no one in particular, and began to pace to and fro restlessly, slamming the clenched fist of one hand into the other. 'Whoever's done this will be up before the super, and may God have mercy upon their soul. I wouldn't fancy their chances of lasting in the Service. This leak could jeopardise our whole operation.

'Wherever the man is, he'll have it on his toes, now he knows that we've got something on him. Who would be stupid enough to give him a tip-off like that? I'll have their guts for garters, before throwing them to Devenish.'

Her temper had barely cooled when they left the station and separated to go to their cars. By the time they left them, however, just outside the Hardys' cottage, she had got herself more in control, much to Lauren's relief. She'd rather spend the evening in an unsecured house than with Olivia in a filthy mood, she had decided, having recently suffered from Kenneth's own foul temper.

The sight of Hal's beaming face, though, cheered the DI, as usual, and her expression cleared like of storm clouds disappearing from the horizon. Hal had cooked up a roast dinner, and the three of them, along with a rather wan Ben, all sat down to eat in cheerful mood.

As the plates were cleared away, Olivia suddenly exclaimed, 'Damn!'

'What is it, my sunshine?' asked Hal before Lauren could get her mouth open.

'I haven't been able to get an answer from Hibbie's phone. I wanted to give her a ring because she's been gone for so long. but I can't actually pin down the date when she said she was going to spend with this friend. I don't even know where her friend lives. I'm so distracted these days!'

'Give her office landline a ring tomorrow. She ought to be in work, and while she can reject or ignore your calls on her mobile the landline should catch her. That way, you should be able to nail her down. And if that doesn't work, I'll drive over to her office and have a word, face to face,' he said in a reassuring voice.

'Dear Hal. You always have the answer for everything. I'll stop worrying, then.' Olivia was all smiles once more. 'And Lauren and I are going to play our flutes again tonight,' she informed the company at large.

'Can I go to Eric's?' asked Ben. 'You approve of him, and he only lives just down the road. I could go on my bike.'

'And I'm playing at the club again, so that should work out to everybody's satisfaction,' finished Hal, who not only cleared the table but also loaded the dishwasher before he went out, his final task being to open a bottle of wine for 'his girls'.

'I'll see you later,' he called as he left.

Ben wasn't long in following him out of the door and Olivia commented, 'Rather them than me. It's brass monkeys out there. I'd much rather be in here before a roaring fire, playing duets and drinking wine.'

'Me too,' seconded Lauren, putting her flute together and getting out the music stand that she now knew her boss kept behind the settee. Olivia disappeared over to the sideboard and came back with a box of dark chocolate mint wafers.

'I get these in towards Christmas, but I can't think of a better use for them than to cheer us two up,' she said.

'My favourites.'

'Mine too. Let's have another go at that jig to see if we've improved since last time.'

They hadn't, and Olivia got out her small tape-recorder again. 'Just to see if we're making the same mistakes,' she said, switching it on, but she really wanted them to record it again for added entertainment when they ran out of puff. Olivia knew well the sheer hilarity of sight reading being recorded, but only because she was a fairly inaccurate sight reader herself – and Lauren was her match. Even though Hal played his steel drums, he simply didn't have the complexity of fingering needed to play the flute, and couldn't really see why the two women found their enthusiastic ineptitude so funny.

In a break between two sections, Olivia asked her sergeant what was going to happen with Kenneth.

'I've asked my solicitor to issue him with divorce papers. In fact, I got in first, because he was solicitor to us both, and now he won't be able to act for Kenneth. That'll really annoy him, having to find a new solicitor. I'm sure he won't even try to contest it, because he's taken Gerda with him and will be openly living with her on site, with all the company witnesses to their liaison.'

'How do you feel about what's happened, now it's had a day or so to sink in?'

'It was inevitable that we'd split up,' Lauren replied, looking thoughtful for a moment. 'Living at a distance for so much of the time had driven us apart, and we had nothing but the children in common anymore. It just so happens that Gerda was the catalyst. She's only a reaction to the fact that we haven't got the relationship we once had, and I expect he'll drop her like a hot potato if anyone else more attractive comes along. Poor girl! I almost feel sorry for her now, just being his catspaw. And she'll be abandoned far from home, without a friend to call her own.'

'But you said the two of them had been carrying on for some time.'

'He was always going to cheat with his high sex drive and she was just convenient. I'm sure he didn't think things would go this far, and now he's stuck with her.'

'You sound very certain.'

'I am. And I'm not going to tell the children just yet. There's no need for them to know anything until after Christmas. Time enough then to tell them they'll be going back to the local church school. And as for Christmas, I've spoken to my parents, and they said that the children and I can go there for the celebrations.'

'Won't Kenneth object? Where do they live?'

'Kenneth hasn't a leg to stand on, and they live in the Cotswolds, so he'll have to book into a hotel if he wants to see them and it's going to cost him an arm and a leg,' Lauren uttered, following it with a slightly inebriated giggle of black humour which she just couldn't suppress. It was her turn to have the whip hand now!

At 10.30, Ben came in and went to go straight up to his room, sighing with mock disapproval as he saw his mother opening another bottle of wine. 'Remember that alcohol is an addictive drug,' he reminded them with a hollow laugh, at which point his mother flicked at him with the tea towel which she was using to protect her hands from the cold surface of the bottle.

'You do, and I'll phone Childline,' he quipped.

'You do that, and they'll hang up on you. You're too old for that now,' Olivia replied, smiling at how her son seemed to have bounced back, even though he still didn't look particularly healthy. 'Why don't you get yourself a big glass of fruit juice – and there are bananas in the fruit bowl,' she called to him, pleased when he headed for the kitchen before finally making it to the top of the stairs.

'God, you must be so relieved to have him back,' said Lauren, reaching for her newly filled glass.

'I really thought we were going to lose him,' replied Olivia, holding up her glass in a toasting gesture. Still, all's well that ends well.'

Hal arrived home just as they were listening to the evening's recorded musical efforts, and giggling away like a couple of naughty schoolgirls. 'Hal,' called Olivia into the hall. 'I've developed a sudden allergy to F sharps, and Lauren doesn't seem to be able to play B flats. What do you think of that?'

'I think,' he replied, entering the room, 'that that can't be the same bottle of wine I opened for you before I went out.'

'Spot on, squire,' replied Lauren boldly.

'My, we have relaxed, haven't we,' was his retort, as he headed for the kitchen to heat up the leftover roast potatoes and vegetables. He was starving, as he always was after playing for the evening.

'I tried Hibbie's mobile in my break,' he informed them through a mouthful of semi-masticated food. 'It was just in case she had the hump with you for some reason, but would be willing to speak to her dear old dad,' he finished with a gargantuan swallow, immediately conveying another loaded forkful towards his mouth.

'And?'

'And she didn't answer me, either. I'm beginning to wonder if there's something wrong.'

'I think the best thing to do would be to leave it to me to phone her at the office tomorrow,' Olivia said. 'At least she'd have to be polite if there are other people present.'

'I wouldn't put it past her to say "wrong number" and just hang up.'

'Well, we'll just have to wait and see, won't we?' To Lauren, she said, 'I reckon we ought to be going up now. All hell will have broken loose with Trussler's name appearing in the local paper, and we need to pick up his three henchmen as swiftly as possible.'

'And I need to check when I can move back to my own house. It's very kind of you to put up with me here, but you would be the first to admit that it's not the same thing at all as having your own space.'

'Granted, but you know you're always welcome.'

'Confucius say that guests like fish: after three days they start to stink,' stated Lauren, lifting her arms and comically sniffing her armpits.

'Point taken,' agreed Olivia.

'And you've already had enough to worry about with Ben. Now it looks as if there might be a problem with Hibbie, it would be best if I left you to your own devices.'

'It's a good and very perceptive friend who knows the right time to leave,' added Hal. 'No offence meant.'

'None taken.'

Shortly after nine o'clock the next morning there was a call for Olivia from the landlord of The River View, with information that really made her ears prick up. As she ended the call, she called Lauren over and gave her the gist of what the man had said.

'I was right about putting out that photograph with Genni Lacey made up to the nines and dressed in her trendy clobber. He recognised that all right: it's the only way she'd ever have got into a pub, and it seems like she did get into The River View. The landlord remembers serving her and asking for her ID – she, of course, had one which, with the benefit of hindsight, was obviously forged.

'He knows Trussler and his cronies by sight, and reputation and saw the man himself giving her the old chat-up line, then he saw them leaving together. He said he was concerned for the girl's safety, but, knowing Trussler, he just wanted something to put on the grapevine so that it got to Mary Mackintosh's ears.

'All four of our suspects were in there. Apparently the other three gave him a two- or three-minute lead, then they left as well. What do you think of that?'

'Would he be willing to identity them if we put together a line-up?'

'No problem. He doesn't want elements like that in his pub. It's quite a well thought of place, and the likes of those four just lower the tone.'

'Let's get the troops out and pick them up, then, and we'll see what we can do about getting other bodies to make up the lines.'

Liam Shuttleworth was again dispatched, together with Lenny Franklin, a face they all recognised from their criminal pasts and treated with a modicum of respect. Lauren was getting better at expressing herself now, and gave it as her opinion that anyone who didn't respect the considerable height and bulk of PC Shuttleworth must need their heads examined.

'After what this lot has done, I think they need their bumps felt anyway. And they won't want to raise young Liam's inner monster, if I know them at all,' replied the inspector with a wink.

'He doesn't turn green and break out of his clothes, does he?' asked Lauren, returning the wink with a smile.

'You wish,' Olivia returned, and then watched Lauren's face as it gradually turned red. 'You're such an easy target!'

Their banter was interrupted by a call from the back of the room. 'I've just been speaking to Forensics, and they've matched the identity of the man in the river with the national database.'

'Can you get them to email it to me?'

'Will do, guv.'

'Groves?'

'Yes?'

'Why do you call me "guv" sometimes?'

'Because every time I call someone "ma'am", it makes me think of the Queen. You don't mind, do you?'

'Not at all. I was just curious, that's all.'

'Thanks, guv.'

'Although ma'am is more correct.'

'Yes, ma'am.'

Hardy perused her most recent email to learn that the body in the river was a Daniel Fishburn. He had lived in one of the tiny flats created when the four-storey terraces of once-grand Georgian houses on the seafront had been divided up in the sixties and seventies. They'd just have to high-tail it round there to have a look at the place, she thought, and get in touch with the owner to see if he could enlighten them about the activities of Mr Fishburn.

'Come on, Groves, time to pay a visit to the former home of our rather soggy Mr Fishburn,' she called, picking up her jacket from the back of the chair. 'Appropriate name, in the circumstances.'

'Don't joke about it. You'll make me hurl,' replied Groves, using a euphemism she hadn't uttered since her boarding school days.

Fishburn's flat was as they'd expected. It was minuscule, furnished with obviously second-hand furniture, but fairly clean and tidy. In the wardrobe were some rather flashy suits and ties, and it seemed, from the amount of skin and hair care products they found in the tiny bathroom, that he was a bit of a dandy as well.

'Fancied himself,' muttered Lauren, knowing the signs from Kenneth's toiletries and clothes.

'The ladies would be very disappointed in him now,' muttered back Olivia.

They returned to the living areas of the property. 'I've found a notebook in his bedside drawer,' called Lauren in a somewhat louder voice. 'It's full of notes which seem to be about "getting in on the action" – whatever that means.'

'Let me have a look. I think that could hold the key to why our Mr Fishburn ended up as fish food.'

Olivia held out her hand, took the notebook and began to flick through the pages, eventually sighing as she lowered the source of information on to the bed top. 'That explains a lot. I'm surprised they didn't do this place over before we got here. It would appear that Fishburn was trying to muscle his way in to the local drugs scene. Someone took offence at that, and that's why he had to be deleted. I expect he'd found out a bit too much, and they couldn't leave him breathing, in case he breathed a word to the wrong person.'

'That was a bit harsh, wasn't it?'

'Par for the course with these guys. If you know more than you need to, then you're dangerous and have to be eliminated.'

'But ... why did someone make all those silent phone calls, then set my house alight?' asked Lauren, completely changing the subject.

'Dammit! I'd forgotten we had a mole. Whoever it is has obviously found out your address by illegally accessing personnel files, and passed it on. I suppose my place is never empty, and they must have learnt about Kenneth and Gerda.'

'That sounds like someone's been watching my house.'

'Probably.' Olivia's reply was curt. 'We'll have to get a car to check on you every couple for hours. Can't afford to lose a partner in flute-playing, not to mention a pretty amenable sergeant.'

'Thanks ... I think.'

INTERLUDE

In an anonymous semi-detached house, a man was packing a holdall with everything he would need to get by for the next few days. He had relatives in Wales to whom he could make an unscheduled visit. It would definitely be unhealthy to hang around here for any longer. He'd had enough of being questioned by the police, and he didn't think he could survive another session. Although he considered himself a hard bastard, he was not unmoved by what he had taken part in, and was finding it difficult to live with himself.

It would be OK if it had just been the three men, but what they had done to the girl was unforgivable. He needed somewhere far enough away to get his head together. If he didn't crack, chances were that one of the others would. If necessary, he could disappear from his stopover in Wales and change his name: go somewhere else to start a new life.

Once packed, he took a last look around the house that had been his home for so long. It had never looked much; hadn't seen a coat of paint or new wallpaper for most of that time. The carpet had been the one already down when he and his ex-wife had moved in, and on which his children, when young, had spilled drinks and much worse. The pattern was now barely discernible through the patches of filth. The furniture was also not up to much, being outdated, cheap, and utilitarian.

Everything had been such a struggle when his wife was there. When she left, the children had been old enough to go their own ways, and he had hardly noticed his surroundings. It was just somewhere he watched television and slept, and now he'd never see it again. It had not been much of a life but, as he looked round now, he felt he'd give everything to have had the chance to go on living here, anonymous and unnoticed. He might even have done a bit of decorating.

CHAPTER TWELVE

It was gone one o'clock when they got back to the office, and Hardy immediately began to curse. 'I was supposed to phone Hibbie's work this morning, and they'll be closed for lunch now.'

'They must have an answerphone you could leave a message on. If you leave your rank on the message someone's sure to get back to you.'

'Good idea, Watson. I'll do just that thing, and do it right now.'

As she ended the call, the two PCs who had been sent to bring in the four suspects came into the office to say that one of them had done a runner – Mervyn Lord. Trussler had still not returned home, according to his partner, but they had the other two, and were awaiting their briefs who were, apparently, on their way to the station.

'Get an all ports warning out about Trussler and Lord, and let me know as soon as our two potential canaries are ready to do some singing,' she ordered them. 'Oh, and get the landlord of The River View in here to look at some mugshots. We could arrange an identity parade with the two we've got, but you'll need the electronic photo album for him to identify the other two. We'll get these bastards if it's the last thing I do. Bring him straight to me – or, rather, take me straight to him when he comes in.'

Hardy's attention was fully occupied until somebody brought her a very slim edition of the local paper put out as a special, this time with the headline *Body of Man Found in Sack Identified*. Without a thought for who heard her, she shouted out, 'There's a traitor in our midst!' Not trusting herself to keep any further outbursts in, she clamped shut her mouth, and got Groves to follow her out into the corridor where it was more private.

'We've got to find out who's leaking all this information. We'll have to think of a way of entrapping whoever it is,' she said in hushed tones. 'There are certain things that we need to conceal from the general public so that we don't hinder our own investigations. If everyone knows the details, then we'll have a lot of nutters confessing, but if only we know the facts, then only the real culprit can disclose this withheld information.

'Come on, then, we've got to get on to those two men and re-question them, in the light of their disappearing cohorts.'

First up was Teddy Edwards, a young man who had not quite outgrown his teenage arrogance, and still lived at home with his mother and several siblings. He sat at the bare table in the interview room idly chewing his finger nails, his brief beside him, looking very unhappy.

After the formalities with the announcements for the benefit of the tape, Hardy began. 'We think it's about time you came clean with us, Mr Edwards. Two of your mates have done a runner, and it looks like they're going to leave you and Mr Stoner to take the rap.' She knew she was lapsing into cheap TV speak, but thought it might be easier for the man to understand. He wasn't the sharpest knife in the box – more of a spoon, really.

'My mates would never run out on me,' he stated baldly.

'Well, Dennis Trussler and Mervyn Lord have. That just leaves you and Steve Stoner to take the whole blame for four murders. You'll never see the light of day again.'

'I ain't saying nuffink. I hardly know Trussler and Lord, and I've got loads of other mates.'

'I'll be needing you for an identity parade later on, and we'll see what you have to say after that.'

'An identity parade? What for?'

'You'll see, soon enough.'

'I ain't done nuffink. I just told yer!'

'Only God can see the colour of your soul.'

This was such an unexpected remark that Edwards looked down at his chest, as if he expected to see that invisible part of him on show for the world to see.

The man's solicitor put a reassuring hand on his arm at that point, as he seemed to be getting agitated. 'Just relax, Mr Edwards, and stick to what we agreed.' The witness sat back in his chair and seemed to slump into an attitude almost of unconsciousness.

'Did you know a Mr Daniel Fishburn?' asked Groves, taking over the reins.

'No comment,' replied Edwards, a smile twitching at the corner of his mouth. They had rattled him, but he'd got himself back in control now. *Bum!* thought Groves.

'Did you leave The River View public house on the night Genni Lacey was abducted, in the company of Dennis Trussler, Mervyn Lord, and Steve Stoner with a young girl in tow?' Hardy continued.

'No comment.'

'Did you murder Daniel Fishburn in the boatshed on the east bank of the river, just up from the marina?'

'No comment.'

Hardy was deliberately dodging her questions from one part of the investigation to another, in the hope of catching him out, and she thought she'd seen a flicker in his eyes when she mentioned the boatshed. She really must chase up Forensics on that.

After another forty-five minutes of the utterly predictable session, the duty sergeant put his head round the door and called her out.

'What is it? It had better be good.'

'We can't get enough people of a similar build for the identity parades, but we think we can manage it for tomorrow,' she was told.

'If that don't beat all. There are more shady-looking characters in this town than you could shake a stick at, but today, they all seem to have gone to ground. All right. If you can't beat 'em, join 'em. Get me two lots of men for first thing tomorrow morning, and we'll bring these two back in. This one's brief was already going on about us not having enough to hold his client, so I'll just have to request that he doesn't leave the area, and we'll pick him up again after he's had a good night's sleep.'

As they were leaving the station, Olivia suddenly stamped her foot in frustration and exclaimed, 'Bugger!'

'What is it, guv?'

'Hibbie's employers never got back to me. It's too late to go back in and ring them again. I'll just have to leave it for now. By the way, when's your house going to be habitable again?'

'Not till tomorrow at the earliest, and I should be grateful for that. I emailed Kenneth and told him about it, and it looks like, as usual, he's pulled a few strings to get things sorted out as quickly as possible.'

'He has his uses then?'

'Yes – but they're few and far between in my opinion.'

CHAPTER THIRTEEN

Fate dealt Detective Inspector Olivia Hardy a cruel blow that evening when her mobile rang at about eight o'clock. Hal and Lauren halted their chat as she answered it, then fell silent as she began to bluster and her face drained of colour. After only a couple of minutes she ended the call, let the hand that held the phone drop into her lap, and simply stared into space, silent as the grave.

'What's up?' asked Hal, rising and moving over to sit beside her on the sofa. 'Who was that, and whatever did they say to upset you so?' By now, quiet tears were streaming down her face.

'I just don't know what's going on anymore,' she said quietly. 'That was the manager from Hibbie's office. He said she hadn't been in work for over a week, and he hasn't heard anything from her. He'd assumed she was ill, but then I left that message on the answer service at lunchtime asking them to get her to ring me. She's gone, Hal. She's not here and she's not in work. I wonder if she was ever at that friend's at all?'

'She must have been, if she's only been missing from work for a week. She's been gone much longer than that.'

'How could I not have noticed how long she'd been gone? How was I content with just the odd word on the phone or a text? I've been trying to get her for the last three or four days and she's not answered her phone or replied to any of my texts.'

'Have you got the number of the friend she was supposed to be staying with?'

'In my handbag,' she replied, beginning to scrabble in

it. 'Why didn't I know the exact dates of half term? What sort of mother am I who doesn't even notice that her son is taking drugs and her daughter has run away from home and abandoned her job?'

She was suddenly reduced to helpless sobs. 'First my son nearly dies, and then my daughter disappears, and where am I? At work, of course, totally absorbed in what's going on there, instead of making this house and everyone who lives in it my priority.'

Suddenly she sat up straight, her face a mask of horror. 'You don't suppose *he*'s got her, do you?' she asked, staring at Lauren.

'Who?'

'That evil bastard, Trussler. You've already been a target. Your address and phone number were probably supplied by our mole. What if the slimeball ran into Hibbie and he found out who she was? He could be holding her now, doing all sorts of unspeakable things to her, and we wouldn't know anything about it. I'll kill him if he has laid so much as a finger on her. I'll kill him with my own hands! I'll put out the lights in his eyes and send the bastard to hell!'

'Don't fret like that, Liv,' cut in Hal. 'Give me the number of her friend and I'll ring her. Mothers can be very scary. Maybe she'll be more willing to speak to her friend's dad.'

She handed over a crumpled piece of paper, and added, 'It's that Sadie – you know, the one I don't like because I think she's sneaky.'

'She'll be putty in my hands, you'll see,' Hal assured her, and went off to the kitchen to make the call. He didn't want an hysterical Olivia breaking in on his quiet questioning.

Lauren went over to take the place next to her, seating herself in the space vacated by Hal. 'Chin up. It'll probably turn out to be a storm in a teacup,' she chided.

174

Hal was gone for over ten minutes, and when he came back, he held up a finger to quell the questions already spilling out of his wife. 'Let me tell it without any interruptions,' he said in a firm voice. 'There's no point in speculation without knowledge and facts.'

Lauren put an arm around Olivia's bulk while Hal told his story. 'She was staying with her friend – at first. Apparently there's this lad – no, no, Liv, don't interrupt me, or I shan't go on. He's quite a few years older than her. They wanted to move in together, but she knew we'd say she was too young. While she was staying with her friend, she and this lad made their plans to run off together. When the plans were ready, off they went. That must have been about the time she stopped answering your texts, Liv.

'She told her friend that if we got in touch, to say nothing, but she felt too guilty about that, and had to tell me what little she knew. They said they were going to London, and that they wouldn't be back. She hasn't heard anything from them since, and if we hadn't phoned her, she was going to ring us tomorrow: that's how bad she was feeling about what Hibbie had done to us.'

'What's his name?' asked Olivia, strangely calm.

'Michael,' replied Hal.

'She'd been mentioning a Michael rather a lot before she went. Hal, how are we going to find her?'

From just outside the door, a young voice spoke. 'I heard all that. Leave it to me, Mum, Dad. I've got contacts who were friends with both of us. If anyone can get to the bottom of where she is, it's me.'

'Ben, come in and join us,' invited Hal.

'But you'd better leave any investigation to the professionals,' his mother warned.

'They wouldn't have a clue. I'll wager a tenner that I find her before them. I know her. I know her friends, and my friends know them too. We'll ferret her out.'

'Ben, I thought I knew her. I thought I knew you, too, but that hasn't helped me lately. I don't seem to know either of you, and I'm ashamed of myself for concentrating too much on my job, and not enough on my children.'

'You know I was slipped those drugs. You know me almost as well as I know myself. Hibbie's sixteen, which is a very difficult age for girls, I've heard, and she thinks she's in love. That alters everything. You haven't ignored or neglected us. We've both been very stupid in our own ways.'

Olivia was silenced by the maturity of what Ben said, and Hal cast an admiring eye at his son for the backbone he was displaying. 'Anything you can do will be most appreciated, son,' he said, breaking the small silence that had fallen over them.

'I'd better get into the office and file a missing person's report,' stated Olivia, rising from her seated position, but Hal immediately took her by the shoulders and pushed her back down. 'You're going nowhere now. You can get a good night's sleep first, and tackle it fresh in the morning, and I want no arguments about that.

'Come on, Olivia, take one of your magic tablets, and we'll both tackle this together tomorrow,' said Lauren sensibly. 'At least we know she hasn't been abducted, we just don't know where she is right now.' Olivia had no choice but to obey, though not without a small revolt.

'I'm going to call it in tonight before I go up. It'll mean that things will get going tomorrow a bit earlier, and give them a march on the hunt for her.'

'Do you really have to, Liv?' asked Hal, a look of concern on his face.

'I won't get any rest if I don't at least get the ball rolling.'

The next morning, Olivia was frantically hurling papers out of her bureau, looking for a fairly up-to-date

photograph of her daughter when there was a ring on the
doorbell, and she went to answer it, totally amazed to see
the uniformed figure of PC Shuttleworth on the doorstep.
'What on earth are you doing here?' she asked. 'You
haven't found her already, have you?' Her face gave away
the fact that hope had awakened.

'No, ma'am. I'm terribly sorry, ma'am, but someone
had to come,' he spluttered, nervously shuffling his feet
with discomfort.

'Had to come for what?'

'To look, ma'am. It's procedure. Nothing personal,
ma'am.'

'Shuttleworth, whatever are you burbling about. Come
in and tell me coherently why you're here.' Olivia was
feeling the beginnings of frustration at his seemingly
unconnected ramblings.

Hal's deep voice behind her made her jump. 'I expect
he's come to search the house to make sure we haven't
murdered our daughter and concealed the body somewhere
about the premises,' he pronounced. 'And don't worry,
Constable, we won't take it personally.'

The inspector was whey-faced as the implications of
what was happening sunk in. It was something she simply
hadn't thought of, and its reality shocked her. This was
something they did to other people, not something that
happened to her.

'I-I'm sorry, Liam,' she stuttered. 'It simply didn't
cross my mind that this would have to be done. Come in
and go where you must – but I won't vouch for the place
being as tidy as it should be.'

'That's not my place to comment, ma'am. I'm just here
on orders, so if you wouldn't mind …'

Olivia finally thought to stand aside to let him in, and
Hal showed him the stairs and asked if he'd like to start up
there. 'Just do your job, Constable, and ignore us. Olivia's
well aware of what needs to be done before you can begin

to search elsewhere.'

Olivia had fled to the kitchen where she could have a good cry, which was how Hal found her. 'There, there, baby, don't upset yourself. You know, more than anyone else, that this is just routine.'

'I know,' she sniffed, blowing her nose into a piece of kitchen towel. 'It's just that it's my daughter, and my house being searched for her body.'

As Hal put his arms round her, Lauren entered the kitchen and said, 'I just bumped into Liam Shuttleworth on the landing. He's not boarding with you or anything, is he?'

'He's searching for Hibbie's body,' shouted Olivia, suddenly furious at the hand fate had dealt her. 'Sorry, it's not your fault. I just can't believe that this is happening. What have I done to deserve this?'

'It's nothing you've done ... and it's nothing you haven't done either,' said Hal, seeing Olivia about to butt in. 'It's just bad luck that both of our chicks chose the same time to rebel against the nest. Don't blame yourself. All that will do is render you useless for doing what you should be doing, and that won't do anybody any good, least of all the good people of Littleton-on-Sea, who rely on officers like you to keep them safe in their beds.'

'But I've got to stay here today,' she countered.

'This is the last place you should be. I doubt they'll find her today, so the best thing you could do is go in and get on with nailing these bastards who have been murdering people, including an innocent teenager,' Lauren advised her. 'Come on, let's get going. They'll be in touch if there's any news or progress.'

When they reached the station, news was just coming in about a body found on the end of the pier. It was a bizarre discovery by a surveyor who was looking over the old structure as part of its regular off-season maintenance. He had seen what appeared to be a figure right at the end of the pier, one that seemed to be fishing from a deckchair, and he'd wandered down to say hello and comment on the weather, a necessary part of English culture.

When he'd got to the deckchair, he said something about how cold it was for the time of year, but got no answer. Going round to the front of the chair to see what had so engaged the man's attention that he did not answer, the surveyor had found that the rod was attached to the man's underarm with tape, and there was a neat bullet hole in the centre of his forehead. He was not merely distracted by his fishing; he was stone cold dead.

The man had wasted no time in reporting this matter to the police. As Olivia and Lauren sat down at their desks and were informed of this grisly discovery, the surveyor was being delivered to the station to make his statement, and the body had been identified as that of Dennis Trussler.

'Well, there goes our only suspect on whom we had forensic evidence,' said Lauren with chagrin.

'Too bleedin' right,' agreed Hardy. 'We'll have to get the other two jokers in again for questioning. One of them has got to break sometime, and maybe this is the thing that will get them singing. It's got to be a punishment killing. I said all along that this was tied up with drugs, and that that accident we went to together was somehow involved in all this. We've got to get to the bottom of it before someone else is killed.

'Has anything been heard from the hospital to let us know how our Mr Hanger is? Sergeant?'

'No. I'll give them a ring now, see if he's come round again.'

INTERLUDE

In a shabby room above a business on the seafront, a man was clearing out what served for his office. He removed several sheaves of paper from files and started to shred them. When he'd done that he took a bundle of other papers down the back stairs to the yard and burnt them. Back upstairs in the office again, he removed all personal items from his desk – including a pistol – then took a duster and wiped every surface that he could have touched. He wouldn't get caught with that old one! This took quite some time.

When he'd finished, he packed up the last bits and pieces from the top of his desk and phoned his cleaner, an old lady who lived a few streets away, and told her to come in early today and give his office a good polishing, as he was likely to be subject to a snap inspection from above.

These trivialities dealt with, he donned a coat with a high collar that he turned up, then a slouch hat that shadowed his face, before leaving for the railway station. He'd soon disappear in the anonymous streets of the capital ...

CHAPTER FOURTEEN

Hardy was of a mind to let them stew for a couple of hours, but before she'd decided on exactly how long, there was a phone call for her to go up to Superintendent Devenish's office immediately, if not sooner. 'What the hell have I done now?' she asked of nobody in particular, wrinkling her nose in distaste at the thought of visiting their resident dragon.

'Perhaps he wants to know if you need any more officers to help with the investigation,' suggested Lauren hopefully.

'There!' replied Hardy, pointing out of the window. 'Is that a flying pig I see? I think not, oh naïve one. More likely, he wants to bawl me out for not solving the case sooner.' She could not have guessed in a million years just exactly what was on Devenish's mind this morning, however.

More nervous than she cared to show, she popped into the Ladies' on her way and ran a comb briefly through her hair, then renewed her lipstick, pulling down her blouse and skirt to disguise any wrinkles, before reluctantly climbing the final flight of stairs to the superintendent's lair. She knocked the door somewhat uncertainly, and jumped when the summons to enter came.

'Good morning, sir,' she greeted him, her face a blank.

'Good morning, Inspector. Please take a seat,' came the reply. Devenish was rather like a shark. His face showed little expression until he pounced, whereupon it became as animated as a cartoon character's. He then returned to impassive again once he had finished chewing his victim into easily swallowed pieces.

'I have summoned you here,' he began, 'to ask you about your team's progress on the unfortunate run of violent murders from which the town has recently suffered. Please give me your verbal report, DI Hardy.'

Hardy cleared her throat, which suddenly felt like sandpaper. 'We have forensic evidence due from the boatyard, sir, which will, I believe, link all four of the men suspected of the murders to the killings. These, we believe, took place at said boatyard, and should produce bloodstains, even if these traces are very small.

'We also have reason to believe that the man who was seriously injured in a car accident on the day before the first victim was found is tied in with the murders, all of which are drug-related. I, personally, shall be visiting him in hospital again to see what further information I can get out of him.

'Of the four men we suspected of carrying out the killings, one has been reported found dead, apparently fishing at the end of the pier, but I've got a hunch that that was a planned assassination rather than a pure and simple murder. It has all the signs of a professional job, from what I've heard and could be seen as a punishment from higher echelons for doing a shoddy job, in that we're on to them, sir.'

'Good work,' said Devenish, with a glint of steel in his gaze, before continuing. 'I'd be grateful if you'd get all the evidence and reports to my office by the end of the day, and stand down from the investigation.'

Olivia was poleaxed by this request.

'But … why on earth would you want us to do that? We're pretty close to cracking it.'

'Because you are treading on the toes of another investigation much more important than this one, and it takes priority. There are members of another team who are undercover, and have been for some considerable time now, and we need *not* to blow their cover, and to leave them a clear field to wrap up this case.'

'But that's not fair!'

'Fair or not, DI Hardy, I have my orders, too, and I have to comply. Don't think that these men will be unpunished, for they will be brought to justice, but simply not by us.'

'By whom, then? Sir?'

'Inspector, this is on a need-to-know basis, and you, simply, do not need to know. You'll just have to have faith in my judgement and that of my seniors.'

'But you just can't switch me off like that. It's not fair to me, and it's not fair to my team.'

'I can and I have. Consider this case closed as far as you are concerned. Now, I don't want you to go near it anymore. Disobedience will result in disciplinary action for you and for anyone else who assists you. Do I make myself clear?'

'Yes, sir,' replied Hardy sullenly.

'Before you go,' he added, as she was already halfway out of her seat, 'I have been apprised of your personal circumstances, and consider it my duty to order you to take three days' compassionate leave. You can't think straight with such a situation preying on your mind, and I like my officers to be one hundred per cent focused on the job in hand.'

'But I don't need any leave. Work helps to take my mind off …'

'Hardy, that, too is an order. Get your things and go home. I don't want to see you hereabouts for at least three days. You are dismissed. And, by the way, you can release those men you're holding.'

Hardy left the superintendent's office, her lips clamped shut to avoid saying anything she might regret, and feeling that there should be smoke and flames issuing from her nostrils. She couldn't remember ever being this angry before. And just as they were getting somewhere.

When she got back to her office, her face was like a thundercloud, promising nobody any good. She announced loudly that there would be no ID parade for now, as the super had pulled the team off the case and passed it to higher echelons, and thanked them for all the hours they had put in. She then took time to explain to her sergeant exactly what had just happened in more detail. Groves was as appalled as the inspector was at the injustice of the situation, but managed to persuade Olivia that her time would be better spent looking for Hibbie.

'I'll push from this end, and you can spend some time phoning round her friends and asking her colleagues at the office whether she said anything to them about her plans to disappear.'

Hal had volunteered to go over to the office where their daughter had worked, taking Ben with him. If Hal couldn't ferret anything out, maybe the seductive charms of Ben could triumph where he had failed, and Olivia had to be content with that for now.

Olivia checked on the way out of the station whether there had been any progress or sightings of her daughter, but the answer was in the negative, so there was nothing to get her hopes up about.

Olivia had managed to speak to the friend that Hibbie was purported to be staying with, but she had to wait until she got back from school. The girl said that Hibbie had stayed with her for a couple of days, but that was only so that she and her boyfriend could make plans.

'His name's Michael, and he's about ten years older than Hibbie,' the friend told her.

'And what does he do?' asked Olivia, hopeful that this may give them a sniff of a trail to follow, by contacting his place of work.

'He doesn't do anything. He's unemployed and living on benefits.' This was bad news.

'Do you know where he lives?'

'Not really. He just drifts around sofa-surfing. As far as I know, he doesn't have a place of his own. Hibbie said they were going to disappear in London.' This just got worse.

'When did you last speak to her?' This was her last hope.

'Last night. She said they had been dossing on somebody's floor until they got together the deposit for a place of their own.'

'So, they've got no money?'

'Michael was always broke, and Hibbie used to sub him until he got his benefits.'

Olivia ended the call in tears. Things couldn't be worse. Hibbie had planned the whole thing just to be with this boyfriend, one who couldn't have sounded more unsuitable: he was basically homeless, living on benefits and Hibbie's hand-outs, and had persuaded her to run off to London – at least, she assumed it was his idea. Already she didn't like the sound of him, and although Hibbie had mentioned his name she had not placed any significance on it. She had picked up no clues. Or had she just not heard what her daughter was telling her?

When Hal and Ben got home, they had no more information than she had, but Ben had got a date with the girl in the office who was closest to his sister. 'You never know, Ma, I could turn out to be the new Sherlock Holmes,' he joked, but soon wiped the smile off his face when his mother burst into tears again.

'I feel as if the heart has been ripped out of me. How could a child of mine do this to me – to us? When have we ever seriously stopped her from doing anything she wanted? The closest we came to being strict was when we put time restrictions on when she came in at night, but we let her stay over with friends whenever she wanted. I thought she was happy, getting her own way about leaving school and going to work. Obviously I was wrong, and now she's punishing us for something we don't even know we did.'

Hal tried to comfort her, while Ben did his best to produce a scratch supper using only the microwave and the frying pan, but it wasn't until Olivia had drunk two or three glasses of wine that she managed to stop weeping.

Ben disappeared up to his room to do some mixing, using his headphones so as not to cause a disturbance, and Hal sat with his arm around his wife, trying to change the subject. 'I didn't get the chance to tell you, but there was a bit of an uneasy atmosphere at the club last night.

'I don't know who rattled their cage, but the manager and his assistant were really jumpy, forever disappearing to make phone calls and going outside for a smoke. I thought they'd both given up, but they were both back on the fags last night. For all I know, it might even have been weed.'

But Olivia didn't even have the enthusiasm to pretend to be interested. 'Hal, what does it matter to me what's going on there now I've been dragged off the case? Even if I could tie that place into what I've been working on, nobody would take any notice of me because I've been shut down. Canned. Retired from it.'

'I'm sorry, Liv, I just didn't think.'

CHAPTER FIFTEEN

Olivia didn't wake until midday, having drowned her sorrows in a lake of wine then swallowed down a couple of sleeping tablets. When she did wake up, her mouth was so dry it could have been made of wood, and her head ached abominably as her stomach roiled in protest at the amount of acid that had formed in it.

She managed to stagger into the bathroom and swallow two glasses of water, before putting two large tablets into a third glass. While they fizzed, she got out a couple of painkillers and washed them down with the still effervescent liquid. Then she looked in the mirror and reared back from what she saw. Her hair made her look like a bag lady, and her face seemed to have aged ten years overnight. Her decision to get straight into the shower was a reaction to what Hibbie would think of her if she were to come home today. She needed to look at least human for whenever her daughter came back. She simply couldn't allow herself to go to pieces physically.

When she got downstairs, Hal was in the kitchen cooking some brunch. He told her Ben had gone out really early to check out some of his contacts in the bigger town where Hibbie had worked. He said he'd phone in at regular intervals to let them know if he'd made any progress, but Olivia was like a cat on a hot tin roof. 'I can't believe the stupid girl said she'd go to London. It's an evil place, she could get sucked into drugs, or prostitution just to get together enough money for food. She could get herself killed, Hal, or worse.'

'What could be worse than being killed?' asked Hal.

'Getting hooked on drugs, sucked into prostitution, and getting a regular beating from her pimp. Is that bad enough?'

'God, you really know how to look on the bright side, don't you? What if she gets fed up with living on somebody's sofa or floor, cheesed off with no money and not enough to eat, and all the things she's had done for her like cooking, cleaning, and laundry are suddenly her responsibility. You really don't suppose she'd just turn up here voluntarily, or at least phone and ask for help,' he suggested.

'And what if she's got no money to top up her phone with? She's only got a pay-as-you-go because we didn't want her running up big bills like her friends were.'

'Liv!' Hal shouted. 'You sound like Chicken-Licken when he said the sky had fallen on his head. We can't live on what ifs. *What if* she just decides to get in touch with us and ask us to come and get her? You know our Hibbie; she doesn't like roughing it. She even refused to go camping when the rest of us wanted to go because she couldn't use a proper shower or her hairdryer.'

'I'm sorry, Hal. I guess I've just got an over-active imagination. It goes with the job.'

In the police station, an elderly lady who had come in to speak to somebody of senior rank was passed on to DS Groves. She was in a state of heightened emotion, and gave her name as Elsie Trussler.

Lauren showed her into an interview room and asked her what the matter was. 'It's my boy. Your lot came round yesterday and told me he was dead – shot. Now, I know he wasn't a saint, but he didn't deserve that, I'm sure. But he's been mixing with some rather unsavoury characters, and I warned him, no good would come of it; and now he's dead.'

'And you want us to find out who did it?' asked the

sergeant.

'Oh, I know who's responsible for it, even if he didn't pull the trigger.' The woman's face was grim.

'You do? Who?'

'A man called Julian Church. He runs that big club on the seafront – The Shoreline – but my Dennis started doing odd jobs for him, and he got me my job as a cleaner there. Anyway, my Dennis got into some serious stuff with some other men, and he wouldn't tell me anything about it, just that the money was good.

'I'm no fool, and I can put times and places together. I know him and those three goons he hung around with were mixed up in them killings that have been taking place. Of course, I wouldn't have said anything, only there was this knock on the door, and suddenly my Dennis was dead.

'Well, that man from the club, he phoned me yesterday morning and told me to come in and give his office a right good polishing, which was odd as I didn't normally clean his office, but before I could get round there, I had a visit from your lot.

'As I said, I'm not stupid, and it sounded to me that he wanted me to go and polish away any stray fingerprints. He'd probably given the place a going over himself, but he sounded rattled, and I guess that if he was the belt, I was the braces, and he was going to make a run for it with no evidence left behind to identify him, because of my little can of polish and my trusty duster. It's easy enough to change your appearance, but I do know fingerprints are impossible to alter. They're what are referred to as "irrefutable evidence", ain't they, ducky?'

Lauren couldn't agree more, and took down Mrs Trussler's statement herself, then contacted Devenish's secretary to see if the superintendent had a minute to spare for her, because she'd got some evidence that she thought ought to go straight to him. She was quaking when she finally mounted the stairs, because she had had little to do with the man, but was more than conscious of his reputation of ripping junior officers to ribbons.

He kept her standing, as she explained what had happened with Mrs Trussler's visit, and pointed out the opportunity to go over the club's office before its regular cleaner got in there. The man sat stony-faced while she explained that she had the woman's statement with her, which he took without a word, then informed her that it would be passed to the 'relevant department', before dismissing her without a smile or a courteous word.

'Just keep your nose out of this one,' he said as she exited his office, relieved that the ordeal was over with. 'Those three men's deaths will be paid for without any interference from you or your well-meaning but short-sighted inspector.'

That evening, Ben didn't get back until nearly midnight, to find both his parents sitting fretting about where he'd got to, and whether he'd found out anything further about his sister's disappearance.

'Where the hell have you been?' asked Olivia, her face ashen.

'Give me a chance, Ma, I've just walked through the door. Anyway, you could have phoned me to ask for an update.'

'We didn't want to disturb whatever you were doing,' replied his mother. 'Come on, did you find out anything?'

'Let me get a cup of tea and I'll tell you,' Ben replied, infuriatingly.

'I'll get it. You sit down and tell your mother what you've discovered,' said Hal, rising from his seat. 'I'll make us all one.'

'Come on, come on,' said Olivia impatiently. 'Did you or did you not find out anything?'

'I found out where she really is,' declared Ben with some triumph. 'She's not gone to London at all.'

'Thank God for that,' replied Olivia, putting her palms up to her face, one on each cheek. 'Where is she, then?'

'Down Portsmouth way. Apparently Michael's got family or friends, or something, down there. They wanted to get a place of their own, but Michael hasn't got a decent credit rating, so they couldn't pass the financial checks, even with Hibbie working.'

'Whereabouts down Portsmouth way? Have you got any more detailed information?'

'I haven't exactly got an address, but I have an area covering a few streets where she probably is,' he said, going over to the computer and pulling up a map site. 'I'll print it off for you so you can see.'

'So what have you been doing all day, son?' asked Hal, coming through from the kitchen with a loaded tray.

'I had some early visits to make, then I had some calls to make. After I'd stopped for some lunch, I had some later calls to make, then I took that girl out from the office and milked her for everything she had. She was like putty in my hands.'

'I'd rather you didn't go into details,' commented Hal.

'Did you get her mobile number?' asked Olivia, more prosaically.

'Of course I did, Ma. What love machine would be worth his salt if he didn't get the babe's number?'

'Give it here. I want to ring her.'

'Liv, it's much too late,' Hal cautioned her.

'It's never too late,' she said, punching in numbers on her mobile. 'Hello, I don't know your name but this is Hibbie Hardy's mother, and I'm going out of my mind with worry.'

When the call had ended, Olivia looked like she had been struck. 'Apparently she told this girl that life was hell at home, and that she needed to get away. She and Michael loved each other and wanted to live together without us interfering. How could she say all that when we didn't even realise her relationship with him? We still don't know his surname.'

Taking the map that Ben held out to her, warm from the printer, she looked imploringly at Hal, who shook his head emphatically.

'No, no. There's no way we're driving down to Portsmouth now. We need to get a good night's rest so that we're ready for a long, hard search. It may only be a few streets, but it could take hours to find her. And what if she's not in? We wouldn't recognise this Michael if we tripped over him. No, you're going to bed now, and we'll talk it over in the morning.'

Olivia fleetingly considered driving down there herself straight away, but soon dismissed it. She knew she would be too tired by the time she got there to be of any use searching through the dark sleeping streets.

She was eager that they got an early start the next morning, but Hal put on the brakes even before they'd retired for the night. 'You know Hibbie,' he stated. 'She likes to be busy, and if I know her, she's already got a job, even if that waster who's lured her away from us isn't working. We'd be better going later in the day, we'd be more likely to catch her at home.' The last two words stuck in his throat, as Hal's mind shouted that this was her home, not some anonymous terrace in Portsmouth. He'd had a look at Google Maps and he could see that it was not a salubrious area.

Like Hal, Olivia had to be content with waiting, but she went huffily off to bed convinced that she wouldn't sleep. The stress had exhausted her so much, though, that she was gone even as her head hit the pillow.

It was early afternoon when Olivia and Hal set out the next day, Ben in the car too, as he and his sister had been very close at one time, and his powers of persuasion might prove better than that of their parents, considering what she had told her colleague at work about her home life. It might have been fiction, but it had to come from somewhere, and they had to find out what had caused her to get into such a state that she had run away like this.

There were about six streets in all that made up the area indicated by Ben's source, and all had names like Ladysmith or Mafeking – evidently products of a bygone age and, as they discovered, mostly in a state of disrepair that would lead, not too far in the future, to demolition and redevelopment. It was not an area that had been adopted by young professionals, prettied up and modernised. It was just a neglected corner of this city that, it seemed, nobody cared about.

They parked the car outside a Cash Converter shop, and each of them took two streets to nonchalantly stroll down, looking for any signs of Hibbie, but there was nothing to indicate that she had even passed through.

After twice swapping routes so that they wouldn't be seen traversing the same two streets more than once, they headed back to the car for a cup of coffee from a vacuum flask that Olivia had prepared before they left. She had also made a few rounds of sandwiches to keep them going, and handed these round to the other two.

'Now, don't get downhearted,' said Hal. 'She may be out at work. We'll keep watch from here where we can see down this main road, and if she hasn't appeared in an hour or so we'll do our little reconnaissance trip again.'

'And if nothing comes from that?' his wife asked anxiously.

'Then, we'll start knocking on doors to see if anyone's noticed her coming and going.' For now, there was nothing else they could do, and Olivia felt frustrated with helplessness. Somewhere, out in those mean dingy streets, her daughter was sleeping and living and eating and drinking, and Olivia didn't have a clue where.

About forty-five minutes later the leaden sky began to weep rain. It wasn't a lazy, gentle rain, but one that stung with its iciness and threatened to turn to sleet. It matched Olivia's mood precisely, as she got out of the car again to recommence her hopeful trudging.

It wasn't until she had turned into the second of her streets, that she noticed a hunched, sodden figure, trudging exhaustedly down the road though the winter darkness, illuminated only by the street lamps. Her heart lifted: she knew that outline – she would recognise it anywhere. Flooded with joy and success, she quickly noted the number of the neglected property it let itself into, and gathered her troops together for a confrontation.

Dripping and tense as they were, it was Olivia who volunteered to knock at the door, for there was no bell. To their surprise, it was answered by a tall, lean man with long hair and in tatty clothes, who looked like a modern-day hippy. He remained mute, just staring at them, until Olivia broke the silence with, 'We're here to see Hibbie.'

He was in the middle of saying that there was no one by that name there when a cry from behind him of, 'Mum!' sounded, and their elusive daughter slipped through to the front by the simple tactic of ducking under his arm.

Now the man became vocal. 'She's left you and she's never coming back,' he declared confidently. 'She's with me now, and she doesn't need or want you anymore.'

Completely against the run of his statements, Hibbie threw herself into her mother's arms, and drew in her father and brother, clinging tightly to them as if they were saving her from drowning. Then, without a word, she pulled herself away and stood next to Michael, who put his arm possessively around her shoulders.

'She's made her choice, and she's with me now. She doesn't want to live with you anymore. She's like a little bird that needed its freedom,' he said with a maddening grin of triumph on his face.

'Are you working, Little Flower?' asked Hal, his face

serious and concerned.

'I've got three jobs,' she said with an air of defiance.

'What do you do?' Olivia had decided to leave this bit to Hal, who could remain calm more easily than she could.

'I clean in some offices from six to seven thirty; at eight thirty I start in a local factory, and I get off at five. Then, at seven, I go on shift at a local pub.' She was definitely defiant.

'Well, at least ask us in for a cup of tea and a sit down after we came all the way down here'

As she stood aside to let them in, she said, 'We haven't got any tea. Or coffee,' and just shrugged her shoulders. 'I've got to get something to eat before I go in for my shift,' she added, heading for what was evidently the tiny kitchen.

'Then I'll come through for a drink of water, if you don't mind,' announced Olivia, scurrying after the tiny figure of her daughter, shoulders bowed, her head sunk down on to her chest. She could hear Hal back in the bed-sitting room asking Michael what job *he* did.

Taking the opportunity to be alone with her daughter, she firstly opened the wall cupboards to see what sort of food stock she had in, only to discover a lone packet of rice, a packet of noodles, and a tub of gravy granules. 'Is this all the food you have?' she asked, incredulous. Hibbie had always been very fussy about what she ate.

'We haven't got any money,' the girl answered in an exhausted voice. 'We had to find a deposit for a place of our own before we could move in, and everything I'd earned went on that.'

'And what does Michael do while you're working three jobs?'

'He's unemployed at the moment,' she replied defensively.

'I asked what he did, not what he didn't do,' Olivia shot at her.

'Oh, Mum,' Hibbie wailed. 'He just sits around watching cartoons on the television.'

She rushed into her mother's arms, to be enfolded the way she used to be when she was younger. 'Hibbie,' crooned Olivia softly into her daughter's ear. 'I've tidied your room, changed the bedding, put up a small Christmas tree for you, and Mr Bo-Bo's lying on the bed waiting for you to come home.' She felt that Mr Bo-Bo was a bit of a low blow, one that may have finally lost its power to affect her daughter, but she was wrong.

'I want Mr Bo-Bo,' Hibbie sniffled, like the small child she once was, what seemed like such a short time ago.

'Will you come back with us? I'm sure I can persuade the office to take you back.'

'Yes, Mum, only …'

'Only, what?'

'Can I have a kitten for Christmas?'

'Of course you can,' replied Olivia, breaking the 'no pets' rule that had reigned for so long in their household. 'You can have a baby elephant, if you want, as long as you come home.' Olivia was now in tears, and held on to her daughter as if she would never let her go again.

'I don't fancy a baby elephant,' the girl replied, with a tiny giggle, 'but a kitten would be fabulous. Mum?'

'What, my darling?'

'Can we go home now?'

'Nothing in the world would give me greater pleasure than to bring you home and put all this sordid business behind us.'

'I thought he loved me, and I thought I loved him, but he just wants someone to live with him and pay the bills.'

'That's a valuable life lesson you've learnt. Don't forget it. I don't want you doing anything like this again. It's just about broken your father's heart. It just about killed all of us, especially after what we'd been through with Ben.'

'What about Ben?'

'I'll tell you later, or, better still, he can. Now, come along,' ordered Olivia, still with her arm around her daughter's shoulders.

They walked back into the bed-sitting room and announced to Michael, Hal, and Ben that they would be going now, headed for home. Michael stood up abruptly and whirled round to face the enemy, his girlfriend's mother.

'She's not going with you. She's staying here. We love each other,' he shouted, raising his arms into the air threateningly.

'No we don't,' Hibbie said in a small voice. 'You just want someone to earn the money, wash, cook and clean for you. What you really need is a servant or your mother.'

'Don't you mention my mother,' he screamed, betraying a raw patch in his past. He made to advance on Olivia and Hibbie, but then, Hal stood up, towering over the skinny young man with hatred in his eyes, and a determined expression on his face.

'You will not lay a finger on any member of my family,' he said in a calm but authoritarian voice; the one he had used to control many an unruly class in his teaching days. Michael stopped in his tracks, and Olivia made good her opportunity to rush Hibbie towards and out of the front door, closely followed by Ben and Hal, still looking over his shoulder to make sure that Michael didn't try to follow them.

As he, as last man out, reached the comparative safety of the pavement, a heavy glass vase shot over his head and shattered on the paving stones in front of him. 'To the car,' he shouted, rushing away from the house, the four of them in a tight little bunch. When they were in the vehicle, he started it with all speed, and left the dingy street with a scream of tyres, noticing that Michael had been running down the road after them. The sooner they were out of this neighbourhood, the better.

On the back seat Olivia sat with Hibbie cradled in her arms. 'Why did you go. my little Hibiscus Flower?' asked Olivia in anguish. 'I always thought that you were such an old head on young shoulders, and we trusted you.'

'I don't know, Mum, I just don't know. At the time I thought it was romantic.'

'But why didn't you confide in us? You know we would have supported you if it meant that much?'

'I just don't know Mum,' sobbed Hibbie. her shoulders shaking. 'I don't think I even can talk about it. It's too raw.'

'Whenever you are ready, my love, you know we'll be there for you.'

When they got back to the cottage, Hibbie went straight up to her room and cried solidly for two hours. Olivia and Hal left her to it, knowing that she needed to get it out of her system. When she had quietened down, Ben went up and sat in her room talking to her for the best part of another hour, then Olivia heard her go into the bathroom as Ben descended the stairs and asked what was for supper.

'How is she?' asked Olivia.

'She'll be fine. She's just had a bit of a clash with the big bad world, the way I did, and now, like me, she's come to her senses.'

This was the best news Olivia had had for some time and, vowing that she would spend more time with her kids and less at the station, she went off into the kitchen humming, only to find that Hal had already put a full casserole dish in the oven and was preparing vegetables.

'It'll be ready when we are,' he said, followed by, 'Do you fancy a celebratory glass of wine?'

'I really do, and I think those two deserve one too. This has been a hard lesson for me, but I must get my priorities sorted out before they've flown the nest for good, and my job as a mother is over.'

'Mothers can never retire: their job is never-ending,' he said with a twinkle, a corkscrew in his hand. 'Just think of them in about ten years' time, needing babysitters, someone to take the grandkids for the holidays. You'll be busier than ever.'

'Hope so,' she replied, taking her glass and raising it in a toast.

When Hibbie came downstairs, she was showered and dressed in her most feminine clothes. Her hair was blow-dried into a bob and she had put on a little make-up. 'Sorry I've been such a wally,' she said, lifting her hand up to pat her hair. 'He wanted me to have it all cut off really short, and when I said no, he got so angry that I thought he was going to hit me.'

The shadow of tears appeared in her eyes again, and Hal rushed over to his little girl with a big glass of wine. 'Drink that, my little Hibiscus Flower, and there's one for you too, Ben. We're all back together again, and nothing else matters.' They all raised their glasses to that.

The next day, having informed the station that her daughter was home safely, Olivia again gave the office a miss and spent hours talking to her children asking them about their ambitions, their hopes and fears, and by the end of it, she felt like she had bonded with them again in a way she hadn't since they were quite small. She knew she'd relied upon Hal too heavily, what with his shorter hours out of the house, followed by his early retirement, and she resolved not to let that happen again. Of course, it would, but she'd spot it sooner next time, and put it right before it got out of hand.

CHAPTER SIXTEEN

When Hardy got back to her office, Lauren gave her a warm welcome, asking, 'How is everything. What happened? How did you manage it?' Over a cup of coffee, Olivia unburdened herself of the events of the last few days, her face wreathed in smiles when she got to the bit about Hibbie choosing to come home.

'It was a very harrowing experience, seeing her in such a situation, and by her own choice, too. I just hope she's been sensible and won't announce she's pregnant in a couple of weeks' time. It's all very well running away for love, but you should be very careful who you think the rest of your life lies with.

'That guy was a leech. I checked. He's already got a record for possession of drugs – nothing Class A, but that's beside the point. He'd have led my beautiful Hibbie in a downward spiral until she was living like a pig, old before her time through working several jobs to make ends meet. Do you know what she said he did all day?'

'No,' replied Lauren quietly, unwilling to interrupt the flow, as she knew Olivia needed to get this off her chest to someone not directly involved.

'He sat around eating noodles and watching cartoons on children's television. I don't even know if he could read and write, and from what I've managed to ferret out about him he was from a very dysfunctional family. Our Hibbie deserves better than that. She'll be more careful and not so trusting in the future, I hope.'

'And how are they all?'

'Ben's glad to have his sister back, and he seems to be

fully recovered now, but he's still denying that he took the drugs on purpose. Hibbie seems very light-hearted and cheerful for someone who, only yesterday, confessed to be suffering from a broken heart. And Hal, well, he's in a thoughtful mood, trying to work out how best to protect his chickens without seeming to. Me? I'm just a little bit older and rather wiser, but I'm glad that there hasn't been a real tragedy over the past couple of weeks.'

'I'm so pleased for you all,' replied Lauren. 'I'm glad you're back now. There've been rumours buzzing around here, but nobody knows anything for certain. Devenish is keeping a very tight rein on information, but I believe there might be something in your emails. I'm sure you wouldn't have been cut out of the loop completely because of how much time you've spent on this. People do have some loyalties, and I suspect you've got one or two surprises waiting for you.'

Olivia looked round before opening her computer. 'Have you caught the mole, yet? And where's Colin Redwood?'

'On suspension awaiting investigation.'

'What?'

'He was caught trying to hack into your computer when he heard that you might have copies of emails sent to the superintendent. His mobile was seized, and there were some compromising texts on it, and some phone numbers that pointed the finger to him being our office leak.'

'Good God! I hope he was well paid. He's put his career on the line, and there's no going back.'

'Apparently he has large debts and expensive tastes,' said Lenny Franklin.

'Come on, guv,' said Groves, 'I can't wait any longer. The suspense has been killing me. If I'd known how to hack into someone's files, I might have had a go myself.'

'DS Groves, behave yourself!'

There were indeed a few very interesting and

informative messages on Hardy's mail system, and she pointed them out to Groves, who read them over her shoulder, whistling softly under her breath. 'Well, that clinches it, but we've been pulled off the case,' she said dismally.

'There's more than one way to skin a cat,' replied her boss cryptically. 'I'll talk to you about it later. Good God, I'd forgotten you had been staying with us. Did you get back home? I'm so sorry, but I couldn't think about anything else but this Hibbie business.'

'No worries. Yes, I'm safely back in my own nest, with no cuckoos in it now.'

During their lunch break, safely ensconced in the privacy of Lauren's car, Olivia outlined how she viewed their situation. 'I got an email from Forensics confirming that tiny splatters of blood were missed in the clean-up at the boatshed. They were from all four murder victims. And there were traces from all our four suspects in the mezzanine office. I also got an email about the sweep for fingerprints in the office at the club – Hal said there'd been some sort of fuss going on the last time he played there and, whatever Church believed, he didn't quite manage to eliminate every print.

'Just before we left the building, I had a phone call from Dylan MacArthur – didn't recognise his voice; he'd been away with a nasty dose of 'flu. And he said he'd been an absolute mug and forgotten to send me a supplementary report on Genni's body. He said that the bite marks *could* be matched to the teeth of the suspects. So all we need to do is to get them to bite into an apple and we've got them. That, with the evidence of Genni's blood in the boatshed, should clinch it.'

'But we've been officially warned off,' countered Lauren.

'From the drugs investigation and the deaths of the three men, we have. But, what about the abduction, rape, and murder of a minor? That seems to me to be a completely separate incident. I don't see how the super can moan about us going after the remaining men on that one.'

'He'll tear you to shreds.'

'I don't care. The kids of this town need protecting. No one knows that better than me, at the moment, and I want to see that any dangers that I can identify are taken off the streets and locked up for a very long time.'

'You'll lose either your rank or your job,' warned Lauren.

'I don't care, right at this very moment. I've been very close to losing both my kids recently, in one way or another, and I'm starting off the rest of my life with my priorities right. If Devenish wants the guilty to get away with things, then he's going to get no co-operation from me. Those men are as guilty as hell of four murders. If I can only get them done for one, then I'll be satisfied. I expect the books will be balanced when the Drugs Squad winds up its operation. If not, at least I've got those responsible for what I see as the worst of their crimes – stealing the life and future from a young girl, and devastating a respectable family unit.'

'What about our drugs courier – Hanger, the man still in hospital?'

'The Drugs Squad can vacuum him up themselves. He'll talk when he's conscious again, and maybe even that list of names he had will turn up in the wreck of his car when Forensics have finished with it. He's not our birdie anymore.'

'And I've remembered where I saw that Mary Mackintosh before, guv. She was up on a drugs charge at my old station.'

'Look her up and send the information upstairs. It's not on our agenda anymore,' replied Hardy, with a sneer of scorn that they had been cast aside so easily when they were so close to the truth.

'You reckon they'll mop up the whole drugs operation in this town?'

'As much of it as they can, without risking the lives of their undercover agents too much.'

'For someone who's got as many years as you under their belt, you still have a touching faith in law and order.' Lauren couldn't help herself.

'I'd leave, the day I realised that had died. I need that belief to keep me going, month after month, year after year.

Anyway, I'm going out now.'

'Where?'

'To buy some apples.'

'You're mad.'

'I know, and bad, and dangerous to know. You get Shuttleworth and one of the other Uniforms to round up our remaining two suspects, and I'll be back to tempt them. No doubt the Drugs Squad will also pick up Mervyn Lord, wherever he's hiding out. Us? We're just about finished.'

An hour later, DI Hardy was informed that Teddy Edwards, aka Woggle-Eye, and Steve Stoner, aka Flinty, had both been picked up and were in a holding cell waiting for her attentions.

It hadn't been an easy hour for the DI, and she had spent it mentally berating herself from getting so far away from her children that she couldn't see what was right under her nose. She could, now, recall conversations with Hibbie about some guy she'd met and wanted to buy a present for, and also noticing that Ben had come home a couple of times in a state that she could only describe as 'spaced-out'.

She'd already spoken to Hal and he'd warned him off pot, especially about smoking it in their family home. Maybe she should have taken him to see some of the recovering addicts at the out-of-town clinic, as Lauren had suggested. They should've used shock tactics on him; come down on him harder, so that they actually had an impact with their moaning, and he recognised that it wasn't just the namby-pamby cotton wool wrapping that he had probably taken it for.

As it was, he'd frightened the life out of himself, and nearly out of his parents, too, and she hoped he would not leave the primrose path again after his brush with death. If Hal hadn't gone upstairs when he did that night, they'd have probably found him dead in his room the next morning, and she'd be visiting his grave by now.

As for Hibbie, they were lucky that Ben had been able to find out what he did about her whereabouts. If he hadn't done that, they may never have found her, and God knows what might have happened to her. She and Hal had nearly lost everything.

Of one thing she was certain, however, and that was that she was going to charge the men responsible for the abduction, rape, and murder of Genni Lacey, and see them behind bars, if it was the last thing she did in the police force – service, she reminded herself, with a wry grin.

Completely irregularly, she had the two men taken into an interview room together, with Lauren and Shuttleworth present.

When they were seated across the desk from her, she passed them each an apple, much to Shuttleworth's consternation. 'Would you two gentlemen please bite into the apples, then pass them to me,' she requested, as they looked at each other in perplexity. Neither had enough brains, in her opinion, to blow their noses if their brains had been made out of dynamite.

Crunch!

Crunch!

She would feed herself to Devenish later, and he'd have

to make up his own mind what to do with her. For the moment, all that mattered was getting justice for an innocent girl.

CHAPTER SEVENTEEN

The next day Hardy drove into Littleton-on-Sea in sleety rain, knowing that a chewing-out awaited her. When she got to the office, Groves was sitting at her desk looking rather queasy. 'What is it?' the DI asked, concerned.

'I had a call from Kenneth,' Groves answered briefly, then stared into space again obviously distracted by something.

'And what did he have to say for himself?'

'He phoned to apologise for the anonymous calls. They were all from him, egged on by the ghastly Gerda. She thought it would be funny to put the wind up me, and he went along with it because he was so angry about us breaking up like that.'

'They were all him?'

'Yes, but it still doesn't explain who set fire to my house, does it? Whoever did that is still out there.' The sergeant was evidently very worried that the culprit would return and try again.

'We'll get him, whoever he is,' her boss assured her, but without much inner confidence.

Suddenly, the phone on the inspector's desk shrilled, and she answered, her face immediately taking on a grim expression. She listened for a short while, said, 'I'll be right up,' and ended the call.

'What's up?' asked Lauren, looking concerned.

'Devilish Devenish wants me upstairs again. When I get back, could you apply the bandages and sticking plasters? I just hope this bollocking doesn't involve donning a uniform again and going back to walking the beat.'

'Stick up for yourself. You've done nothing wrong, and you can always call me up to support you?'

'Fat lot of good that would do. I'll just have to convince him that I'm on the side of the angels.'

Hardy mounted the two flights of stairs slowly, her insides churning at what was to come. Devenish didn't take any prisoners, and he would not look kindly on what she had done; how she had handled things.

Standing to attention at his desk, she felt her heart in her boots, as he began berating her for her actions on the Lacey case. 'I gave you a direct order to stand back from the investigation. The next thing I hear is that you have arrested Edwards and Stoner.

'What on earth did you not understand about standing away from the case; standing down your team and leaving well alone?' His top lip was curled in a sneer, his brow furrowed with creases of anger.

'I didn't disobey a direct order, sir.'

'That's a blatant lie,' he roared.

Gathering her courage in both hands, she continued, 'I stood my team down as you ordered, sir. I then had some further information from Dr MacArthur, sir. This indicated to me that the abduction, rape, and murder of a minor had nothing to do with drugs, sir.

'I treated this as a totally separate case, sir, and carried on with my enquiries. I feel that there is enough forensic evidence to put away Edwards and Stoner – and Lord, when he is caught, sir, with respect.'

'Hardy, although you are *really* trying my patience, I want to know if you have anything else up your sleeve.'

'No, sir. I was just doing my job as I perceived it, sir.'

'Inspector, you are obdurate, devious, and uncooperative, but I cannot find fault with your persistence. Though maybe it would be a good thing to rein in this part of your personality in the future.'

Hardy stood silently.

In the void that followed, Devenish continued, 'I find you insubordinate in the extreme, but I've got my eye on you now. If I see you put a foot out of place at any time in the future, I will have your rank, and bust you down to a uniformed constable pounding the beat again. Do I make myself clear?'

'Yes, sir.'

'Get back to your duties, but don't forget that I am watching you very carefully.'

'No, sir.

When the inspector left his office she found that she was shaking all over, and that there were tears in her eyes – tears of fury. If she'd asked him if he'd like two dangerous murderers left free to roam the streets of Littleton-on-Sea, he would have thrown a hissy fit, saying she was implying that he didn't police his patch properly, although she knew it would have been true. She had absolute belief that what she had done was right, and that she shouldn't be criticised for trying to put such dangerous men behind bars.

She had not trespassed on to the drugs aspect of the case. She had merely worked round it, seemingly risking her career for what she perceived as good policing. Damn the superintendent, and his ilk, more concerned with their own skins than the safety of the public whom they were supposed to protect.

She couldn't seem to get a balance in her life. She felt she had neglected her family, given the way her children had behaved recently but, at the same time, she felt she would have been neglecting her duty had she not acted as she had, with regard to Edwards and Stoner. At the moment she couldn't seem to do right for doing wrong. Damn them all. She needed someone to talk to, and somewhere else to do the talking.

Back at her desk, as she removed her coat from its hook

and put it on, Groves rose and joined her. 'Where are you going?' she asked.

'Off to play hooky in the coffee shop. Are you coming? I could do with a sympathetic ear.'

'You try and stop me,' replied Lauren, grabbing her own elegant cashmere jacket. 'I've got some good news for you.'

Settled with a coffee and a Danish pastry in front of each of them, Lauren was asked to impart her good news by a sceptical Olivia. 'There was a call while you were in the dragon's lair, which I took for you.'

'About?'

'The new forensic evidence about the bite marks has cemented things, and the file has gone to the CPS for approval to prosecute, and the men are being held until a magistrate's appearance in the morning to remand them in custody.'

'That's the best news – workwise – that I've heard in a long time. Here's to a successful prosecution,' said Hardy, holding up her coffee cup. 'And we can arrange that ID parade we never had for the landlord of the River View.'

Two days later, it was reported that Mervyn Lord had been stopped trying to board the Eurostar to Paris. He had been detained and fingerprinted, and was now on his way to the Littleton-on-Sea station for questioning.

This time, he was so rattled that he confessed in the hope that co-operation would shorten his sentence, guessing what was happening when an impression of his bite was taken. In his attempt to throw some of the blame towards his partners in crime, he also let slip that it was Edwards who had torched the detective's house.

'He was as high as a kite that night, and I couldn't do nuthin' with him. God knows what he'd taken, but he'd had that many lines of coke that you could've got high just from his hanky. He said he wanted to "get" one of the coppers who'd been persecuting him, and he knew where one of them lived because one of the filth had squealed. I told him he wasn't fit to drive, and that he'd better leave well alone, but he got away from me, saying he already had a can of petrol in the boot of his car. I was shit-scared, and decided to leave him to it. I didn't want to be prosecuted for frying a copper. It was him did it, not anyone else; certainly not me. If you don't believe me, have a look in his car. I bet he's still got the bloody thing in there. He's daft enough not to have got rid of it.'

'And you didn't think to phone and warn someone at the station?' he was asked.

'What do you think I am, a grass?' he asked, then reddened, as he realised he was being exactly that at that very moment.

Ten days later, when all three men were awaiting trial at one of Her Majesty's secure hotels, the town exploded with armed police at 5.30 in the morning.

It was a carefully planned raid, with targets being the Shoreline club where Hal regularly played, the Littleton-on-Sea Marina, and a boatyard just a couple of miles upriver. Several private houses were also raided, and a large number of arrests made, as well as a fair haul of illegal substances confiscated. Fortunately there were no fatalities and few injuries.

Julian Church was arrested at a very exclusive residence where he was paying a visit, and would now be paying an unplanned visit to prison, probably for a very long time.

The three men held on the charge of abduction, rape, and murder of a minor had decided that they might as well be hung for sheep as for lambs, and decided to take down with them anyone that they could. Julian Church was the highest up the chain that their knowledge extended.

Evidence gathered from this raid and the resultant arrests ended the no-go area that had been the cases against Lord, Edwards, and Stoner, and those murders could now be added to their charge sheets, along with that of conspiracy to murder against Church.

Peter 'Cliff' Hanger, the man who had been involved in the head-on collision at the outset of this case, never recovered consciousness and died a week after the drugs raid from a blood clot on the brain.

For a while, a short while, peace and sobriety reigned in Littleton-on-Sea.

EPILOGUE

November bled into December. The weather remained cold but was drier than it had been, and Littleton-on-Sea looked very pretty with its crust of frost, decorated shops and festive lights strung everywhere, lit trees twinkling from front windows. The sound of Slade was abroad all over the town, adding to the seasonal atmosphere.

Olivia Hardy, after work one night, sat in her car in the police station car park in a reflective mood. The town sounded good, it looked very attractive, but she knew that under the surface there still existed the dark underbelly of the town, the violence, the criminality, and the law-breaking.

The place was a series of half-healed wounds all just waiting to be scratched for their infection to bubble to the surface again, and for the evil merry-go-round to clank into life once more, its unsettling, slightly out of tune piped music bleeding into the dreams of the innocent and blighting their lives.

The only question was, when?

THE END

Andrea Frazer

Strangeways to Oldham
The Curious Case of the Black Swan Song
Choral Mayhem

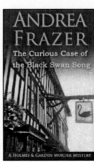

For more information about
Andrea Frazer
and other **Accent Press** titles

please visit

www.accentpress.co.uk